I0788092

THE LORDS OF SUMMER

1986

TRISTAN VICK

A REGOLITH PUBLICATIONS BOOK

THE LORDS OF SUMMER: 1986
Book 1 in The Lords of Summer Series
A Dark Forces of Nature Novella
By Tristan Vick ©2025. All Rights Reserved
www.tristanvick.com

Published by Regolith Publications
First Edition, copyright © September 25, 2025.

Stock Art "Meteor Shower" by: Andy_Art @ Pixabay
Final chapter art by: Christopher Awayan
Cover design by: Regolith Design
Written & Edited by Tristan Vick

ISBN: 9798267464093

Contents

1

1986
PART 1: LORDS OF SUMMER

IT WAS THE SUMMER OF 1986, AND WE DECIDED to make the best of our summer vacation. For Billy, Jimmy, Paul, Mitch, and me, this would be a summer we'd never forget. That was our solemn promise to one another. In a few months, we'd become high schoolers. Some of us would be splitting up and attending different schools. The next time we'd take a test, we'd be miles apart with nothing but the memories of the time we shared. This is why we had promised to make this summer count – to create one final, lasting memory that would stand the test of time.

The school bell rang, and our principal, Mr. Harrelson, stood in the center of the hall amid a sea of moving children, calling out for everyone to walk peacefully. "Walk, people! Walk! Don't run," he shouted over the din of the mass exodus. Summer was finally upon us.

Commotion and chaos ensued as someone lit off some smoke bombs and tossed them into the middle of the hallway. The bold colors of yellow, green, and red flooded the hall, enveloping the fleet of passing sneakers in a thick, multicolored haze. Almost immediately after that obvious diversion, a string of firecrackers exploded in rapid succession – POP! POP! BATTA-POP!

Children screamed and laughed as they spilled out of the front school doors. Mr. Harrelson, our pudgy red-faced principal, stopped at the entrance, threw his hands on his hips, and shouted, "Who lit these firecrackers?"

He received no reply except for the pandemonium of giggles, sneakers squeaking, and multi-colored school bags shuffling away from the crime scene as smoke filled the school corridors. Amidst the parting crowd, we saw Jimmy manifest before our very eyes, a smile stretched wide across his freckled face as he tucked a lighter back into his pants pocket and held his finger to his lips, demanding we keep his little secret. With a wink, he turned and disappeared back into the deluge of classmates.

The mass exodus of sneakers continued outside, and they joined the queue of yellow buses waiting in front of Woodridge Junior High School to ferry the children home.

Sunlight washed over my face as I dashed out the school doors, slid down the railing, passed several underclassmen as I went, and then landed on the ground. Without skipping a beat, I raced to the bike rack as fast as my red and white Chuck Taylors would carry me. Unlocking my bike chain, I looked up in time to catch Billy Bardem shoot me a nod as he came out of the school's doors a few paces behind me. I nodded back, and we paused and smiled, both of us recalling our promise.

Jimmy Polson suddenly erupted onto the scene, leaping down the entire flight of stairs outside the main school entrance. He landed with a thump and sprang up, his red hair catching the sunlight like the flaming tips of Ms. Liberty's torch. He smiled at us, freckles and all, and shouted, "Last one to Billy Bardem's house is a toe-licking, butt-sniffing loser!"

As I hopped on my bike and pedaled furiously down the street, I thought about our summer plans and how our parents were too busy with work and adult things to take fancy vacations like the wealthy families did over the summer furlough. Usually, our summer vacations included more local activities, such as visiting the town pool every day or staying indoors on scorching hot days to play Dungeons & Dragons. But this summer was about us. About living life to its fullest.

Decided by unanimous vote, the entire gang agreed this summer we'd hang out in the forest behind Billy Bardem's house for as long as we had the gumption to weather it. He had a treehouse fort about half a mile behind his home, which we had designated "Fort Liberty."

Billy's parents had inherited eight acres from his grandfather, and where their property line ended, the Glen Forest State Park began. It was the perfect area for a tree fort. A nearby creek provided easy access to fresh water and fishing opportunities. Billy's brother Marvin, whom we just called Marv, had caught some freshwater crawfish a couple of summers back and showed us how to cook them over a campfire at the foot of Fort Liberty's enormous oak and dogwood tree trunks.

Billy didn't talk much about his dad, but we knew that when Marvin and Billy were little, their father had framed the treehouse and got it ready for them. After their dad had passed away, his transport plane having crashed down over Tehran, Iran, in the botched Operation Eagle Claw of 1980, the treehouse sat unfinished for another five or six years. Before Marv graduated from Woodridge High School, he and Billy got together and finished building it. It gave them something to bond over after the loss of their dad.

Seasons come and go, and after graduation, Marv moved to the city for college. Billy finally moved out of the small first-floor bedroom and into his brother's old room in the attic. It was wide open, had Marv's old record player, a pool table, and a couple of beanbag chairs situated around an old color TV crammed in the corner of the room where they'd often play Atari games together.

The rest of Marv's stuff, however, Billy had relocated to the tree house, including a Butane stove for campsite cooking, a fold-out futon bed, three kerosene lamps, lots of fleece blankets, a poster of Cindy Crawford wearing a stars and stripes bikini which hung prominently on the wall inside the fort, and a first aid kit. It had taken us nearly two weeks to move all of Marv's stuff to the treehouse, making small trips where we each carried one item along with our other camping gear. The end result was a fully stocked and fortified base of operations replete with a five-gallon bucket toilet equipped with a fold-down seat cover.

Situated amid a sea of conifers and placed twenty-odd feet up in the trees, Fort Liberty was a proper stronghold and quite likely the most incredible treehouse any of us had ever seen. It was the treehouse out of every boy's dream—except it was *our* treehouse—and none of us took that for granted.

Billy and I had spent many evenings getting up to mischief in this place, his father's old kerosene lamps casting a warm glow over us as we sat drinking orange Crush sodas and looking at Marv's old collection of Playboy magazines.

Deep down in my gut, though, I knew that these retreats were just Billy's way of remembering his father and keeping him close. But for me, the retreat held a different meaning. Unlike Billy keeping the candle in the window for his father's spirit, for me, it was an escape. An escape from the gut-wrenching reality that my father had walked out on Mom, Melody, and me several years ago. While Billy came to Fort Liberty to honor his father's memories, I came to forget mine.

Mom said Dad left because he wasn't suited for family life. But I later learned from grandma that dad was a philanderer and, according to her, a conman. He was a lawyer, but I suppose it was the same difference in my grandma's eyes. Even so, he still sent Melody and me birthday cards with ten-dollar bills tucked inside on our birthdays. That's about as much as we ever heard from him.

High school was looming over us with its promise of girls, first kisses, football games, and parties. But all that seemed like an eternity away. Three months of summer were long enough to forget all our troubles, and something was stirring inside us, and it wasn't just our hormones and acne breakouts either. This summer was destined to be the last hurrah before we looked up to see our youth receding in the rearview mirror of life, each memory a yellow dash along the dotted highway.

For this very reason, Billy and I had assembled the whole crew. Jimmy "Mad Dog" Polson, Paul "The Brain" Anders, Mitch the "Big Mac" McIntyre, Billy "Back Woods" Bardem, and, of course, myself… Travis "Maverick" Mahoney.

All our nicknames held deeper meaning, at least for us. Jimmy, of course, had a temper, which made his name all the more fitting. Paul had a wicked afro, and Mitch was a little on the husky side and loved to eat. However, Billy's nickname made the most sense because he knew the woods outside his home like the back of his hand. As for me, I was somewhat of an odd duck and mostly kept to myself. That is, until Billy befriended me. You see, Billy was the glue that held the whole gang together. Without him, we were just a bunch of silly kids. As a group, though, we were a brotherhood.

My BMX bike's brakes screeched loudly as I skidded into my yard and let the bike fall out from under me. It crashed down onto the lawn behind me as I leaped off, allowing the momentum to carry me up the front porch stairs. My thumbs hooked on the straps of my school backpack, I shot up the steps and swung open the tattered old screen door with such vigor and gusto that I could hear the spring whine in protest before it snapped shut, nearly pinching my bag as I slipped into the house.

Once inside, I heard my mom's voice call out from the kitchen, letting me know we were having pork chops, steamed peas, and mashed potatoes with a boatload of gravy for dinner. My mouth began watering just thinking about it. It was, hands down, one of my favorite meals that she made.

My sister, Melody, was playing with her Barbie dolls as I raced by the open doorway of her overly pink room on the way to my bedroom. She looked up just long enough to log that it was me and then went back to playing with the weird dolls that she'd fitted with her handmade wardrobe of clothes sewn from one of Mom's old leather jackets. All the dolls were dressed in black leather and had a Beyond Thunder Dome aesthetic. I don't think Mel was into the dolls as much as crafting outfits for them. She loved making clothes and had a natural talent for it.

Mel and I got along fine, at least as fine as any other siblings, but we didn't have all that much in common. Twelve-year-old girls like Mel didn't care what big fourteen-year-old brothers like me did in our off time. Other than sitting down for dinner or running outside to the ice cream truck whenever it rolled around, our paths didn't cross often. She kept to herself, and I kept to myself.

Determined not to waste any more time than necessary, I flung my bag onto the bed, my books spilling out of the top flap as I'd neglected to zip it all the way shut after class. I guess I was in a hurry, it being the last day of school and all. It didn't matter much since most of my room was a complete mess anyway.

My room was a stereotypical boy's room. It had a 'Ride the Lightning' Metallica poster on one wall and a blue Lamborghini Countach on the other. My hamper was in my closet, lid up, clothes overflowing as though it was spewing them out all over my bedroom floor. Next to my bed sat my trusty clock-radio, perched on my desk. Its red, boldfaced digital numbers counted down the minutes until I'd be hanging with the boys at Fort Liberty.

Not wasting any time, I opened my duffel bag and began tossing in whatever clothes I found. That didn't necessarily mean that they were clean, just that they were the most convenient. Packing just enough for three nights at Billy's tree house in the woods behind his family's house, I threw in a can of Lowrey's beef jerky, several changes, clean underwear, three pairs of socks, and my army green toothbrush. By 'boy logic', that ought to last a good long month, I thought.

Skkkrrr

"Travis, this is Billy. Do you read me over?" came Billy's voice over the crackle and pop of the RadioShack walkie-talkies that I'd gotten as a present for my eleventh birthday.

Skkkrrr

Fumbling over my feet, I picked up the pile of clothes, tossed them onto the chair next to my dresser, and picked up the walkie-talkie that manifested underneath. Mashing the red button, I replied, "I read you, Billy. I'm about to eat, and then I'll head out. Meet you and the gang at Fort Liberty at seventeen hundred hours. Over."

Skkkrrr

"Roger that, Travis. Don't forget to bring extra marshmallows to make S'mores. Paul is on chocolate detail, and Mitch is bringing the Grahams. Jimmy and I are bringing the sodas."

Skkkrrr

"Copy that. Over and out." I tossed the walkie-talkie into my overnight duffle, landing on a plastic bag of Jet-Puffed mallows stowed inside.

"Dinner!" my mom called out just as I was zipping up my things. I tossed the duffle onto my bed and raced out of my room and back down the hallway toward the kitchen, nearly plowing into Melody, who darted out in front of me, inadvertently cutting me off.

"Watch it!" I said, annoyed that she was slowing me down. I was on a mission, and nobody or anything was going to stop me from meeting up with the boys and having the weekend of our lives—least of all, annoying little sisters like mine.

"You watch it, dumbass," Melody spat back, annoyed by my general existence. We began elbowing one another as we headed down the hallway and into the kitchen before breaking apart and scrambling to our seats at the dinner table.

With great haste, I began snarfing down the food, Melody looking at me with equal parts bewilderment and disgust. I opened my mouth to show her the nasty ground-up contents inside, and she whined.

"*Mommm!* He's doing it again," she griped.

"Close your mouth when you chew, Trav. And,

for God's sake, slow down, slugger," Mom said, ruffling my hair as she leaned over to place the pot of steamed peas on the kitchen table. "I don't want you to choke to death."

"Yeah, chew your food like a normal human being," Melody added. When Mom's head snapped around and she hit her with a chiding gaze, Mel smiled innocently. Quickly disarming any biting criticism my mom was about to dole out, Melody batted her big girl eyes and said, "This is the *best* meal ever! I love you, Mom."

"I love you, too, sweetie," Mom replied with a soft chuckle, brushing Mel's hair behind her ear and gently stroking her cheek with her hand.

Mel's ruse worked as Mom forgot all about what she would say to her and merely smiled at her instead. I let out a disgruntled sigh.

"Love you both to the moon and back," she added, smiling at Mel, then slowly fixing her gaze on me. Parents had to be fair like that, I guess.

That's when I noticed Mom had on perfume. A nice green tea perfume she'd received as a gift from our Korean neighbors, the Kims. They were your stereotypical American Asian family, and he was a dentist, and she was a housewife. I'm pretty sure they didn't have any children either. On the other hand, my mom was a single working mother trying her best to make ends meet. She worked as a night nurse at the Woodridge Clinic. She only took the night shift because it paid thirty cents more per hour. Yeah, I know, a total scam. But she said we could use the extra money. And by that undeniable scent of her perfume, I knew that she was headed to work.

"Hey, guys," she said, sitting between us and reaching over with a fork and knife to cut Melody's food for her even though she was old enough to do it herself, "I've got to go in tonight, and I need you both to…"

"Don't say it, Mom," I pleaded, peas tumbling out of my mouth as I spoke. "I'm hanging with the boys all weekend at Fort Liberty."

Mom shot me a sharp glance and said, "Well, then… you're just going to have to take your sister along, aren't you?"

"Totally unfair," I mumbled under my breath.

"What was that?" Her tone was back to that classic Mother Hen, don't mess with me and do your chores kind of tone that she took whenever we pushed one too many of her buttons. I instantly withdrew my earlier protest.

"Nothing." I turned my face away and folded my arms to pout, but I kept any further comments to myself. Our regular babysitter, Sarah Lewis, the high school girl who used to babysit both of us when we were younger, wasn't available as often these days, and my mom didn't have the time to find a new sitter. I sure missed Sarah, though. She was a blonde-haired, blue-eyed goddess who was on the school dance team, and I think Mel was pretty fond of her as well.

At any rate, the details weren't important. What was, however, was the fact that I couldn't weasel my way out of having to babysit my little sister for the entire weekend. Mom had work, and I was stuck with my bratty, know-it-all sister. That's when I looked up to find her grinning at me from across the table.

"Fine," I said, mumbling additional complaints under my breath.

"Good," Mom said, eyeing me firmly to let me know her final decision.

Then, reaching toward my sister, she grabbed Melody's chin and drew her gaze into hers. "As for you, young lady, don't give your brother a hard time.

He and his friends have been planning this camping trip for ages. You hear me?"

"Don't worry, Mom, I'm your little princess. I'll hardly be an inconvenience."

"Wonderful," mother said, rising to her feet. "That settles it then." Bending over, she kissed Melody on her forehead and then turned back toward me and gave me a reassuring smile as if to say, 'you've got this'. Finally, she scurried over to the coat rack and grabbed her things.

"Mom," Melody asked as she sat patiently, waiting for the right time to spring her question. "Can I borrow a can of hairspray? I want to do my hair up later."

"Not in your wildest dreams, little lady," Mom responded without looking back. She rummaged through her turquoise purse until she found her car keys. "That stuff isn't for kids. Besides, it's highly flammable. I don't want you touching it. Do I make myself clear?"

"Crystal clear, mom," Melody said, her tone only slightly dejected. That's when she shot me another ear-to-ear grin, and I had to do a double-take. I recognized that mischievous glint in her eye and knew this wasn't the end of it. But I also knew it was safer not to ask any questions. The less I knew, the better.

"Alright, you guys," Mom said, her keys jingling as she headed out the back door. You two behave and watch out for one another. We're all we have." She smiled at us one last time before slipping out into the muggy, mosquito-ridden evening, letting the screen door slam shut behind her. Her last words echoed from the backyard, "And don't forget to lock up before you go."

The rumble of the Volkswagen Beetle's motor coming to life was followed by a couple of revs that crescendoed with a pop of the exhaust. Intermittently backfiring as it went, the baby blue bug released smoke signals down the entire street as Mom headed to work. That's when Melody whispered in a menacing tone, "So, big brother, when are we leaving?" She grinned even wider as if to taunt me with her mere presence, and I glowered at her from beneath a thick set of creased eyebrows.

"ASAP," I retorted, sliding my chair back and springing to my feet. "Grab your stuff and we'll hit the road. Oh, and don't diddle-daddle to annoy me, because I will leave you here with nobody to keep you company except for your creepy dolls."

Ten minutes later, she met me at the back door in her jeans and brown long-sleeve shirt with a bulging pink backpack, a yellow fanny pack, and one of mom's old faux gator-skin purses – slung under her arm.

"What on Earth are you bringing?" I asked, noting the obvious—she had packed way more than she needed.

"Amenities," she replied, a puckish grin forming on her lips.

"Whatever, just make sure you have your sleeping bag and toothbrush," I said.

"Got'em," she replied, patting her backpack as she held it in her arms.

"Good. Now, let's get going, because we're a bit behind schedule and we still have to pick up Mitch."

With that, we locked the back door and cut across the driveway to our bikes. Melody's purple banana bike, replete with rainbow handlebar tassels, was propped up against the chain-link fence, and I fetched my silver BMX from the lawn where I'd discarded it earlier. Luckily, Melody had a basket on the front of her bike that allowed her to stuff the giant Allegator skin purse into it.

"You'd better keep up," I shouted over my shoulder as I took off down the street. Determined not to lose sight of me, Melody stood up and peddled as fast and hard as she could. Being bigger, I still pulled away, though, a subtle smile finding its way onto my face as I left her in my dust.

2

1986
PART 2: THE PRINCE

THE SUN WAS BEGINNING TO SET ON THE horizon, pressing hot pinks into hotter oranges as we rounded the boulevard and came up to Mitch's block. Melody and I headed toward the house halfway up the street, only to find that all the neighbors were convening outside on this hot summer night. They all seemed to be enjoying their respective evenings. Mr. Kim sat on a lawn chair in his front yard, beer in hand, as his wife, Mrs. Kim, attended to their flower garden. I waved at them as I rode by, and they waved back.

Further down the road, I saw Mitch's dad watering his lawn with a hose. He seemed obsessed with keeping his front lawn greener than a typical golf course and meticulously tended to it. When he saw me ride up to the house, Mr. McIntyre shouted over his shoulder. "Mitch, your friend Travis is here. You'd better get a move on since it'll be dark soon."

"Hi, Mr. McIntyre," I said, pulling into their driveway. "Is Mitch ready?"

Before Mr. McIntyre could answer me, a voice chirped, "Ready as I'll ever be." Mitch appeared from inside his open garage, wearing his trademark red t-shirt and khaki shorts. His dusty-blonde colored bangs hung in his face, but didn't seem to obscure his vision at all. And although he was portly, I wouldn't exactly call him fat. Just…thick-boned.

His sister Megan was also thick-boned, but she had other assets that made her the talk of our group, often to Mitch's chagrin. Although it annoyed Mitch, everyone in the group was obsessed with Megan's bust size. Nobody was more obsessed with Mitch's sister than Jimmy. Although being obsessed might be putting it too mildly, since he not only talked about her incessantly, but he also cut every single one of her yearbook pictures out of the school yearbook and pasted them up on the inside of his locker.

Mr. McIntyre watched us push our bikes to the end of the driveway, and before we had a chance to get on our way, he cleared his throat and said, "Now, don't go getting into too much trouble. I know how boys can be at your age... getting into mischief and whatnot. I was fourteen once, too, you know." He chuckled to himself and went back to watering his lawn.

"Don't worry, Dad," Mitch said, letting loose an overly dramatic sigh, "We'll be good." As he hopped onto his bike seat, prone to chronic clumsiness, Mitch slipped off the pedals, nearly racking his nuts on the middle support bar of his mountain bike. Somehow, he managed to save face with a quick recovery and his manhood still intact.

No harm, no foul, I thought, a wry smile forming on my face as I shook my head in amazement. Still, I like Mitch. He was loyal and kind. He was a compassionate soul, and he was the most innocent of us all. And it's these defining traits that, I'd argue, were his greatest strengths.

As he clambered back onto his bike, I noticed that Mitch's backpack was over-stuffed with supplies and looked nearly twice as heavy as mine. Its weight practically forced him to the ground as he struggled to regain control of the situation. "We're just going to roast marshmallows and tell stories by the campfire. You know, guy stuff."

His dad laughed again and, in a sarcastic tone, replied, *"Riiight,"* leaving it at that.

Just then, the roar of a 1979 Pontiac Firebird Trans Am coated in metallic-wine paint, screamed by us. It was almost as though the golden eagle adorning its hood was screeching bloody hell as the tires squealed around the corner.

We turned to see which idiot was disturbing the peace of this otherwise blissful suburban evening, only to see Sarah Lewis riding shotgun, her arm hanging out the window as her hand rode the waves of the breeze as they passed us by.

Time seemed to creep to a crawl as she looked over at me, the wind jostling her blonde flowing hair, some of the strands crossing her face. She brushed the stray tufts of hair out of her eyes and tucked them neatly behind her ear, reigning them in, and then smiled at me as the Firebird roared past. In that moment, the world faded, and she was the only thing in my focus—an angel riding shotgun.

Like a dunce, I smiled and waved back, feeling amazed that she still remembered that awkward kid she used to babysit. But then I looked over my shoulder and saw both Mitch and his father waving too, and I realized I couldn't be sure who she was waving at, if not all of us.

I let out a frustrated sigh and turned back to watch her leave. Before we knew it, with the deep throttle growl of the American V8, the Trans Am disappeared around the corner and out of sight, stealing away with Sarah into the sunset.

"So beautiful," I said under my breath."

"They don't make them like that anymore," Mitch said, still staring off into the distance, visions of Sarah Lewis dancing in his mind.

"No, they don't, son," Mr. McIntyre replied. "No, they sure don't." They both nodded as though some sagely advice had been imparted, and I raised an eyebrow, hoping to God that they were talking about two completely different things.

To my relief, Mr. McIntyre said, "I had a '73 Trans Am back in the day before the old ball and chain made me sell it." He chuckled at the 'ball and chain' bit, but then a sadness came over him, his face growing melancholy as he reminisced about the good old days with his beloved car. "Now, that was a gorgeous car."

Once all the commotion had passed, we said our goodbyes and parted ways with Mitch's dad. Starting on our way, Mitch and I rolled out into the street just as Melody eased up alongside us, having taken her sweet time catching up. Mitch shot her a dismayed glance from behind his shaggy blond bangs, his eyes darting back and forth, first to me and then to her and back again.

"Ah, man," Mitch said, sounding more bummed than usual. "I thought this would be a guy's *only* weekend."

"Sorry, man. It can't be helped. My mom has the night shift all weekend long. And I got stuck with babysitting duty."

"Maybe my sister could…" he paused as he thought about how to remedy the situation. He knew that Megan had babysat Melody for extra cash in the past, but with her new job, there was no way she'd be able to work around her schedule. "Nah, never mind. She has work tonight at the bowling alley."

"It's fine," I said. "Just pretend she's not even here. That's what I do."

"You guys know that I can hear you, right?" Melody asked in a less-than-amused tone.

I ignored Melody and shot Mitch a wink. "See, not even here."

He smiled and then looked over at Melody, who merely gave me the stink eye. Something, by the way, I was completely used to. Then, she turned toward Mitch and flipped him the bird.

"What the Hell?" he said, caught off guard by the rude gesture. "Your sister's mean, did you know that?"

I laughed and then rode on ahead, taking point.

Several minutes later, we arrived at Billy "Back Woods" Bardem's house and parked our bikes along the side of his garage. Three additional bicycles were already lined up, evidence that the others had arrived ahead of us.

Going around back, we saw Billy's mom smoking a cigarette from the open kitchen window. She blew out a smoke ring and then, seeing us, waved away the smoke and pointed toward Fort Liberty. "Billy and the others already headed out. You'll find them at the fort."

We turned and looked out at the woods, and sure enough, the white Christmas lights at Fort Liberty were on, letting us know that the rest of the gang was already there and accounted for.

"There she is," Mitch said reverently as if our kid's treehouse was a national treasure.

The thing is, though, I shared his sentiment—we all did. "Fort Liberty, as I live and breathe," I added, finishing his thought for him.

"Majestic," Mitch said. "There's no other word for it."

I nodded in agreement, a couple of bright, beaming smiles pressed onto both our faces as we stood peering out at it as if it were a famous landmark like Mt. Rushmore or the Grand Canyon.

Melody let out an exasperated sigh. "God, you two are a couple of dorks. You talk as though it's your freaking girlfriend. If you love it so much, why don't you marry it?"

"You're still just a kid, so I don't expect you to understand," Mitch said, lecturing Melody, who folded her arms across her chest and stared at him sternly. "Fort Liberty is much more than just a tree house in the woods. It's a haven. It's a place where we can be free of everyone and everything. Adults don't bother us there. We make the rules. Heck, we can say 'no girls allowed' and it's binding. It's our own Never-Never Land. We can do what we want. Eat what we want. Drink what we want. It's absolute freedom."

"What do you mean, I'm still just a kid? *You're* still

just a kid. Also, it's *Neverland*, not Never-Never Land, dipshit. Oh, and answer me this, geniuses. If your stupid rules are binding, then how can it be absolute freedom? What if one of you gets a girlfriend, and she wants to join? I guess you hadn't thought about that. But maybe I'm giving you morons too much credit. It's not like either of you could ever get a girlfriend anyway." Melody laughed at her own diss and then confidently strode off, her head raised high, her nose sticking up into the air, a slight hint of smugness in her step.

I looked over at Mitch, who seemed to be wracking his brain over the question, his logic trounced by my little sister.

"Dude," he said, letting out a sharp exhale. I could see the embarrassment glowing on his cheeks. "That girlfriend thing…that was just mean."

I laughed. "Yeah, she tends to be like that. She'll get under your skin if you let her. But, like I've already told you, you need to ignore her," I replied, slapping Mitch on the shoulder. "It's the only way you'll ever find any peace of mind." Mitch nodded in silence and followed me as we plodded up the trail.

Almost as soon as we entered the trees, dusk

faded to night, and we dug our flashlights out of our bags. The trail was hard to discern, especially at night, but no matter where we were on this hillside, we could always see Fort Liberty—shining her light on the darkness and showing us the way.

"Look!" Melody shouted, hopping up and down with excitement as she pointed at the sky. "A shooting star!"

We all looked up and staggered back with awe. What began as a white streak of a potential falling star grew into a hot, orange blaze. What's more, it grew closer and closer, bigger and bigger. This wasn't any ordinary shooting star; it was a meteor shower.

Our eyes fixed, we watched the large chunk of the meteor's main body break into about a dozen smaller pieces, all of which were glowing red hot as they broke apart in the atmosphere. Then, the whole thing released a thunderous boom that sounded like the jets at the airshow streaking by. To our astonishment, the rocks flew over our heads just as low as the jets did at the airshow, and the meteorites shot over us and past Fort Liberty.

We covered our ears from the noise and watched the closest piece of meteorite sink below the forest ridge line and disappear. A split-second later, there was an even louder boom, and the ground quaked beneath our feet. It was close. Damn close. We shared astonished glances, and our hearts began racing in our chests.

"Holy shit!" Mitch blurted out. "Did you feel that? I think a meteor just crashed down."

"No shit, Sherlock," Melody quipped, and I shot her a sharp glance to let her know to ease up on Mitch. He'd done nothing wrong, but she was relentlessly prodding him for some reason.

"No need to be rude," Mitch retorted.

"No need to be a dipshit," Melody fired back.

"Hey! Don't be a brat," I said, my voice louder than usual. "You know how mom doesn't like it when you snipe at people."

"I can't help being smart," she said.

"A smart-ass, maybe," I teased, smiling and nudging her arm with my elbow to let her know I wasn't trying to be cruel. She just looked at me and then scoffed lightly under her breath, clutching her backpack straps and twisting them irritably in her hands.

"So," I added, giving her a stern look. "What do

you have to say to Mitch?"

"What I want to say is that he needs to go on a diet, because his tits are almost as big as his sisters," Melody said, quick to add, "But that would be mean."

"Melody," I growled through gritted teeth. By my tone, she knew that I was starting to lose my patience with her level of disrespect and rudeness toward my friend. I pointed at Mitch, who looked as though he were about to cry. "Apologize this instant, or you can turn back now, go home, and I'll deal with Mom and the consequences later."

"Alright, alright…" Melody deflected, raising her hands in the air as she turned toward Mitch. "I'm sorry for all the stuff I said."

"That's better," I said, looking over at Melody and Mitch, "The sooner we get to Fort Liberty, the sooner we can meet up with the boys. Then, we'll go check out that crash site."

"Sounds like a plan," Mitch said, shaking off Melody's jabs and taking point.

I shot Melody one final glance to gauge her reaction to having been thoroughly scolded. Seemingly, it was water under the bridge as she merely smiled at me and started down the trail.

I smiled for the victory won and, looping my thumbs through the straps of my backpack, I followed my sister and Mitch down the path with renewed vigor, as the three of us hurried the rest of the way to the treehouse.

3

1986
PART 3: DISPOSABLE HEROES

AFTER SETTING OUR THINGS DOWN AT FORT Liberty, we found Billy, Paul, and Jimmy already eager to check out the meteor. Flashlights in hand, we headed into the woods, ready to climb over the hill to see what we could see. None of us knew what to expect, but we were all itching to find out.

Dry twigs and leaves crunched beneath our feet as we trudged up Woodridge Hill, for which the town gained its namesake. Paul pushed his glasses onto his nose and brushed his fro back, but it bounced back into place. "Hey, Billy, what's on the other side of this hill anyway?"

As we marched up the slope, ducking rogue branches and avoiding loose rocks, Billy replied without looking back. "Nothing much. Just a ton more trees and three or four miles of forest until it meets the old highway that wraps around the adjacent hillside. Once we get over this hill, you'll see across the valley to the Make-Out Point, where all the high school kids go to get their Mack on."

"Hey Mitch," Jimmy said, an excited tone to his voice as he slung his arm across Mitch's neck and shoulders. "Speaking of babes getting their Mack on, your sister said that Sarah Lewis was coming to Make-Out Point with her boyfriend tonight, right?"

"Yeah, so?"

Making the "OK" sign with his hand, he began poking the hole with his finger, crudely gesturing at what teenagers might be getting up to at the lookout point.

Jimmy turned to find us all scowling at him, arms folded across our chests as we shot him our most disapproving gazes. Paul merely pushed his glasses up again and said, "Not cool, man. Not cool."

Unaware of why everyone was suddenly mad at him for a joke he'd made a thousand times before, he threw up his arms and asked, "What'd I do now?"

"Hey, man," Billy snapped, shooting Jimmy a

harsh glare. "Travis's lil' sis is standing right here. We don't need that kind of locker room talk in front of a lady. Watch your manners."

I appreciated Billy's protectiveness of my lil' sis and, more than this, his loyalty to my family. He was like the brother I never had. Even so, his mediation wasn't necessary. Melody was fully capable of standing up for herself. Besides, she had me, too.

When I looked at Melody, she was eyeing Billy with the dreamiest gaze you'd ever seen. "You doing alright?" I asked to make sure. After all, I was her big brother. I couldn't just leave Billy to care for my little sister.

"It's fine, guys," Melody assured us, brushing aside the male prepubescent preoccupation with the female anatomy. "Really, it's no big deal."

Even though she wouldn't admit it, I could tell she was bothered. She just wanted to hang out with the gang. She didn't want to talk about all that stuff fourteen-year-old boys are prone to obsess over. What did a twelve-year-old girl know? She was here because she had no choice. Mom was working. That wasn't Mel's fault.

"Guys," I said, shooting everyone a scowl, "maybe

we can move on from this topic and talk about something else for a bit? Melody doesn't need to hear about you pervert's wet dreams about Sarah Lewis."

"The only wet dreams I have are for Mitch's sister," Jimmy teased, hopping up and down and slugging Mitch playfully in the arm. "Megan's got the biggest rack in all of tenth grade." Jimmy immediately turned to Melody and said, "Sorry, Mel. But it's true. She does."

Melody waved her hand and turned away, as if to say she wasn't bothered. Billy and I just looked at one another with bewildered glances, both thinking the same thing—we pondered how truly thick Jimmy's skull actually was. After all, we'd just lectured him on his uncouth language, and he turned right around and doubled down, as though he was completely unaware of how to act in front of a girl.

"Ew, don't make me gag," Mitch said. "She's fatter than I am."

"Hey," Jimmy said, flashing his trademark grin as though he was going to say something particularly heinous, "don't body shame your own sister, man. That's uncool."

"Yeah, uncool, Bro.," Paul added. He reached out

and poked Mitch's arm with a long finger. The grin on his face spoke volumes. It wasn't that he was actually agreeing with Jimmy so much as he was using this as an excuse to tease Mitch. The two of them have been best friends since primary school.

"Besides, big girls need love, too," Jimmy added, dry-humping the air in mock coitus.

"And *there* it is," Mitch said, pinching off a rather lengthy sigh.

"Okay, everybody, just stop being gross for like half a minute," Melody said, her patience for their ribald banter finally reaching its limit.

While everyone was joking, I had gotten lost in my thoughts and found myself looking around our immediate area. That's when something strange caught my eye. A trail of glowing embers littered the side of the hill that sat directly to the north east of us. "Over there!" I shouted, shining my flashlight at the hillside. "You guys see that?"

Everyone turned and followed my light's beam until they also saw it. "Holy shiznit!" Mitch blurted out. "Is that what I think it is?"

It was the crash site. And, sure enough, a crater about the size of the city swimming pool had formed in the middle of the forest. Our hearts pounding excitedly, we began to race recklessly toward the smoldering meteor site.

Jimmy, in his excitement, raced past all of us and took the lead. "Come on, guys. What are you waiting for? We found it. We actually found it!"

Indeed, we had found it. But what we didn't consider was whether it was safe or whether it might be radioactive. For that matter, we didn't pause to think whether there might be some alien bacteria or something else that could contaminate us and make us all sick or turn us into neon-green nuclear zombies or something.

All we knew was that our feet could barely keep up with the thrumming of our overexcited heartbeats.

"Wait up, guys!" Melody called out from behind us as she struggled to keep up. But we were too invested in the discovery to slow down or care whether or not my lil' sis could keep pace.

About five hundred meters later, give or take, we finally arrived at the impact site. To our collective disappointment, there really wasn't much to see. Just some scorched earth, with char marks on the nearby trees. You could make out precisely where the meteor had crashed down because the pine needles were singed where it cut through them. It had carved a five-hundred-meter path through the trees, and the red glowing embers were of the pine needles and thin branches that had caught on fire from the extreme heat of the meteor. Other than that, it was pretty lackluster. No glowing rocks. No UFO or little green men. Just rocky debris and some smoke.

"Fiddlesticks!" Mitch grumbled. "What a total letdown. There's nothing here but a bunch of rocks." He slid down into the pit of the crater to get a closer look and kicked one of the rocks. It made a strange popping sound and hissed, like when you press a metal spoon to dry ice.

"What was that?" Billy asked. "That noise, just now." He hopped down into the crater, too, and we all looked at one another and then slid down to meet them.

Jimmy, being the genius he is, bent down and picked up the steaming rock with his bare hands. He held it in his palm for about two seconds before yelping and dropping it.

"What?" asked Paul. "Is it hot?"

"No," Jimmy said, spitting on the palm of his hand

and rubbing the saliva in. "It's cold. Colder than a witch's tit."

Billy and I shot each other perplexed glances. Coldness isn't a side effect of falling through Earth's atmosphere. These rocks should be scalding hot. Not searing cold. In fact, the meteor had burned a path in the forest, so how in the world were the rocks that set fire actually ice-cold? We glanced around at one another's baffled faces. We had no idea what to make of all this.

"How can that be?" Mitch asked, turning to Billy. "What does it mean?"

"Beats me," Billy said with a shrug. "I'm no scientist. How should I know?"

"Yeah," Jimmy laughed in jest, "He barely graduated from the eighth grade. How do you expect him to know anything? It's a wonder he can even tie his shoelaces."

"Shut up, dickwad," Billy retorted.

"Bed-wetter!" Jimmy fired off.

"Here they go again," Paul said, a pent-up sigh escaping his lips.

"Butt-licker!" came Billy's reply.

"You kiss your mamma with that mouth?" Jimmy

shot back.

"No, but I kiss yours." Billy puckered up and made 'kissy faces' at Jimmy. "And she likes it!"

Naturally, it was only a matter of time before Jimmy lost his temper, unable to keep flyting at Billy's level. Red-faced, he lunged forward and took a swing at Billy.

Billy ducked out of the way, avoiding getting clocked in the side of his jaw, and Jimmy stumbled past him, nearly face-planting in the dirt. Jimmy caught himself with both arms and popped back up nearly as quickly as he'd fallen. Spinning around, a wild-eyed look on his face that earned him the nickname "Mad Dog," he threw a handful of pine needles, dirt, and dry grass into the air. It all exploded into a dust cloud, but instead of being the grand attack he thought it would be, the dirt and debris merely fluttered to the ground in anti-climactic fashion.

Of course, this caused Billy to laugh all the harder because Jimmy's reaction was so outlandishly comical. Under normal circumstances, Paul and Mitch would be laughing too, but Jimmy was seeing red and, like a shark in the water, was out for blood. Both Paul and Mitch had to jump in and hold Jimmy back, making sure he had enough time to cool down. Luckily, Billy's cooler head prevailed, and he took a step back and threw up his hands in surrender.

"Jeez, man. We both got in some good digs. Learn to take a joke."

"Yeah, man. Calm down," Paul said, shifting his grip on Jimmy's arm to keep a hold on him. "You both said some pretty wild shit. As far as any of us are concerned, you're both squared up."

"Yeah," Mitch nodded, agreeing with Paul. "You were going on and on about my sister's tits earlier, and I didn't try to knock your teeth out."

Jimmy looked down at Mitch and took a deep breath, and then let out a long sigh. "I guess you're right. It's unfair of me to sexualize your sister if I don't at least let Billy sexualize my mother."

"Um, I don't think that's the lesson we should be taking away from this," Paul said, letting go of Jimmy. Mitch did the same. "We shouldn't be sexualizing women."

"Says who?" asked Jimmy, looking around at everyone's faces. Billy, Mitch, and Paul were at a loss for words and merely shrugged.

"I happen to know for a fact that women like the

attention," Jimmy informed, although we all knew he was full of it.

"No, they don't," Billy replied.

"Maybe not when you give it to them. But the ladies go wild when I shower them with my charm. The ladies can't get enough. You should see them falling all over me all the time."

"I'll take your word for it," Billy replied, a dry sarcasm unpinning his every word. He rolled his eyes and then turned to me. Noticing something was wrong, he cleared his throat and said, "Hey, Trav, what is it?"

While they were busy hashing it out, I realized that I hadn't heard from Melody in a while. To make things worse, she was nowhere to be found. My heart sank in my chest.

"Where's Melody?" I asked, turning to the boys and scanning their faces, hoping one of them had some good news for me. But I was only met with blank stares. "Where's my sister?"

"Don't worry," Billy said as he motioned for everyone to spread out and canvas the area. "We'll find her."

Everyone fanned out and began searching for her

when we finally found her standing just beyond the apex of the crater, staring out into the distance. But that wasn't the strangest thing. The thing that freaked us all out was the fact that she was breathing extremely fast and shallow, almost to the point of hyperventilating. At the same time, her entire body was frozen with fear. She didn't even dare blink an eye.

Cautiously sidling up to her, I reached out my hand and gently squeezed her shoulder. "Mel," I whispered, "what are you looking at?"

Suffice it to say, my voice was filled with trepidation as I followed her silent gaze out into the woods – toward the Make-Out Point up on the hill.

"Something's out there," she said quietly. Her voice trembled, and I knew she was petrified.

"What do you mean, something's out there?" asked Mitch.

"A monster," Melody replied. Her voice didn't waver. She stated it as plainly as possible, not sugarcoating it. Pretty soon, everyone had climbed up onto the top of the crater and stood next to Melody, looking out across the valley—toward Make-out Point.

Naturally, a gathering of vehicles had accumulated at the Make-Out Point. The city had erected a scenic observation area to spark a greater interest in tourism to Woodridge's more picturesque locations. Instead, all it did was provide the perfect spot for frisky teenagers to convene and get up to a bit of mischief whenever they felt like it.

As we watched the scene unfold, none of that seemed to matter. Besides, it wasn't the glow of headlights that we were focused on. No, we were more focused on the rustling trees and bluish-purple glow that moved through them. It had a dark radiance, like a black light washing across everything with its phosphorescent illumination, and cut through the woods as it made a beeline from the crash site straight toward Make-out point.

"Are you guys seeing this?" Mitch asked.

"I wish I wasn't seeing it," Paul replied.

"Maybe it's just a bear," Jimmy said.

"A blue-glowing bear?" Paul asked.

"Whatever it is, it's moving way too fast to be a bear," Billy said.

"It's gotta be big too," I added, "if it's jostling those trees around like that."

"I want to go back," Melody said. She gulped nervously and wrung the straps of her backpack in her little twelve-year-old hands. She was terrified. "I want to go back to the treehouse, right now."

"Fudge nuggets," Jimmy blurted out, and we all turned to find him staring at the ground. "I hate to say it, but I think Billy's right. It ain't no bear. Look."

He shone his flashlight at the ground, and, bright as day, a set of tracks appeared. They seemed almost reptilian but were much larger—like Komodo dragon-sized foot depressions—which climbed right out from the crater's center into the woods.

"Holy shit!" Paul blurted, quickly covering his mouth when he realized he'd spoken more loudly than he intended. "I think it's an alien," he whispered. We all shot him dubious looks.

"You don't know that," Jimmy said.

"Meteor... Tracks... Blue-glowing thing," Paul responded, his finger darting from the crash site to the tracks and finally to the strange glowing light moving through the woods. "What would you call it?"

"Everyone, just shut up," I said. "It could be a bear, for all we know. Then again, it might not be. But I, for one, don't intend to wait around to find out. I think my lil' sis is right. We turn back now, while we still can, and return to Fort Liberty. We'll hole up there for the night." I turned back to Melody and said, "Let's go."

"Yeah," Billy said, nodding in agreement with me. "Travis and Melody are right. We'd best get back to Fort Liberty, draw up the rope ladder, lock the doors, and batten the hatches."

Jimmy drew out a switchblade and flipped it about, nearly nicking Mitch.

"What the hell is that?" Paul gasped, looking at Jimmy in disbelief.

"Don't worry, you bunch of sissies. If that thing comes our way, I'll carve it up."

"Those things are illegal, you know?" Mitch said, eyeing the switchblade.

"Where did you get that anyway?" Billy asked.

"My dad left it to me," Jimmy replied. "So what?" He flipped it around and folded it back into itself, finally placing it back inside his back pocket. He smiled at everyone with a dopey grin, and we collectively rolled our eyes.

One might wonder what parents in their right mind would give their child a switchblade. It wasn't that Jimmy's father gave it to him, per se. It's what he left behind after he got sent away. Although it wasn't a subject we dared broach with Jimmy because he didn't get his nickname "Mad Dog" for nothing. Let's say Jimmy had family troubles. But, of all of us, only Mitch and Paul still had fathers.

Sometimes, I envied them. An unbroken family is a rarity these days. The 1980s were an age of independence and doing things differently from our parents' generation.

Under normal circumstances, a kid like Jimmy Polson wouldn't have ever hung out with a bunch of dweebs like us. But the fact that Billy and I understood what it was like not having a father around allowed Jimmy to feel as though he had a kinship with us, a kinship he might not have had with a group of kids with perfectly normal, unbroken families. Jimmy had bonded with us during our fifth-grade year and stayed an integral part of the group all the way up till now. It took us all a few years to get used to his big personality, but over time, he'd settled into the group dynamic, more or less.

Melody squeaked. "I think maybe—"

Melody didn't get to finish her sentence as an

outburst of honking horns and car alarms suddenly drowned out her words. Wide-eyed with fright, we all spun on our heels and looked across the valley to see the cars at Make-Out Point all blitzing out.

The vehicle's headlights flashed and shifted as cars were violently jostled around. Amid the indiscriminate blast of horns, there was a loud screeching of metal grinding against metal as cars slid into one another. From our vantage point on the other side of the valley, it appeared as though the various vehicles were being batted around like a pinball in a pinball machine.

One car flipped up into the air and landed on the roof of a 1969 fastback Mustang. It seemed as if their steel frames were screeching in agony with every collision. Rising above all the chaos and the cry of mangled steel were the even louder cries of the teens. Both girls and boys alike let out dreadful shrieks, all of them fearful for their lives as the bluish-purple glowing light descended upon them. And if Paul was right, that something—whatever it was—had come from outer space.

Horrendous cries echoed throughout the valley. Young people scared for their lives shouted for help.

Other than a bunch of silly kids, there wasn't anybody around who could help. Besides, even if we did decide to try and help, we didn't even know what that dim purple glow was, let alone how to fight it.

"Guys," Paul whispered in a low voice, "Turn off your flashlights."

"What?" Jimmy shouted back, only to be met with a collective round of hushes.

"I said, turn off your damn flashlights. I can only assume that thing was attracted to the car lights, and that's why it attacked everyone at Make-out Point. If it is, then it might be attracted to our lights, too."

"Balls," Mitch said, fumbling to turn off his light and accidentally dropping it to the ground. He fell to all fours and batted the flashlight around before finally clutching it to his chest and flipping the off-switch.

Paul's reasoning made sense, so we all turned off our flashlights. Besides, it's better to be safe than sorry.

"How are we supposed to see anything in this pitch-black darkness?" Jimmy asked, blinking several times and scanning all of our dim faces.

"Just give your eyes a few seconds to adjust," I said. "Once you can see well enough, we'll use the moonlight to guide us back to Fort Liberty."

"Stay close, kiddo," Billy said, grabbing Melody's hand and towing her behind him. I was thankful to him for watching out for my little sister. It showed Billy had a big heart and strong character. Of all of us, he was perhaps the most mature.

"Guys," Melody said, her voice trembling.

"What is it, kiddo?" asked Billy, looking down at her.

"The screams. They've stopped."

Melody looked back over her shoulder as we continued up the hill, and I followed her lead. By the time we'd climbed back down into the crater and back out the other side, the screams had all but died out, and the valley fell silent again.

A deathly silence settled across the whole of the valley, and the purple-blue glow over at Make-out Point intensified. To our dismay, the glowing entity slowly turned around and, leaving the carnage of blood and guts and broken down cars, began making its way back to the crash site—back toward us.

"*Umm...*guys," Mitch whispered, his breathing growing incrementally faster and heavier as panic set in. Soon enough, he whipped out his inhaler and dosed himself. After a short pause, he exhaled and finished his sentence. "It's turning back this way."

"Yeah," Billy said. "We see it."

"Don't worry," I reassured everyone, "We've got at least three miles on it. Even if it can run as fast as a cheetah, that still gives us plenty of time to escape."

"No, it doesn't," Paul said, eyeing me shiftily as he nervously adjusted his eyeglasses.

"What do you mean, *no, it doesn't?*" I asked, shooting him a perplexed glance. Granted, I wasn't the best at math, so I'm glad Paul had the gumption to correct me.

"Cheetahs can run up to seventy miles per hour, as we all know."

"Yeah, yeah," Jimmy affirmed, nodding along with what Paul was saying even though it was clear he hadn't the foggiest. "Seventy miles per hour. We all know that. What's your point?"

Undeterred by Jimmy's interruption, Paul continued. "Well, if it were hauling that fast, it would only take..." he paused long enough to count his fingers and run through the calculations in his mind before continuing, "it would only take three minutes for it to get here and eat all of us."

A strange, squishy gurgle cut the lingering silence

as we stood in shock, realizing that we could be alien food. We all turned toward Mitch, who held his rumbling stomach.

"Did you have to add the 'eat us' part?" he said, a squeamish look on his face.

"Sorry," Paul said with a slight shrug. "I'm just going by what I know. And I know that it just had a four-course meal consisting of greasy teenagers. So, we should be fine."

"It's not that. It's just that I'm starving, and my stomach won't stop growling. Thinking about eating makes it worse." Looking down, he touched his stomach to try to quell its rumblings.

"You're thinking about eating people?" Jimmy asked, a mystified look settling over his face.

"No," Mitch said defensively, giving Jimmy a baffled look. "What I meant is…eating in general…gets me to thinking about food…which gets my tummy churning."

"Context," Paul said, placing a hand on Mitch's shoulder, "Context, buddy."

Jimmy laughed and said, "That's why you're called 'Big Mac' McIntyre." He slapped Mitch on his back hard enough to make it sting, and Mitch frowned as he shot Jimmy a curt look. "All you do is think about food."

"That's not true," Mitch said defensively. "I still think about other stuff, too."

"Your sister's boobs, maybe," Paul retorted with a snort. This got Jimmy and him going, and they both broke into a fit of laughter and high-fived one another, their voices carrying into the night.

"*Shhh!*" A voice hushed us, and we all turned to find Melody holding a finger to her lips. "You idiots are going to get us killed by that creature over an account of Megan's boobs? Grow up, you dickweeds!" Melody stormed off as I turned, looked at the guys, and shrugged.

"When she's right, she's right," I said, nodding in agreement with my little sis. Sometimes, my little sister was right. "Besides," I added in her defense, "She probably has the highest I.Q. out of any of us. So, when she gets serious like this, I'd do what she says."

"I'm fine with that," Mitch said in a whisper. "She's a real ball-crusher when she wants to be. I don't want to go up against her when she's like that."

"Ooh, is the big baby scared of a wittle girl?" Jimmy prodded, teasing Mitch.

Paul put his fingers to his lips and hushed us all again, reminding us that this wasn't the time for idle chitchat.

I saw Billy looking back one last time before jogging to catch up with us.

"What is it?" I asked him, recognizing the worried look on his face.

"The temperature is changing. And fast. I can feel it. We need to hurry unless we want to get stuck out here all night. If a fog rolls in, we'll walk in circles until daybreak."

"Billy is right," I said. "We'd best get back to Fort Liberty. That's our best bet at the moment, and it's certainly better than the alternative." I jutted my thumb over my shoulder, and we all turned to look at the lookout point one last time. The eerie silence sent a chill down all of our spines.

"Right," Paul said, turning as he took the lead. "Let's get going." Mitch followed after him, and Melody reached over and took my hand. My feet practically moved on their own as she tugged at me, and we headed back up the hill, making our way toward Fort Liberty.

Glancing back, I saw Billy standing in the same

spot, staring up at the lookout point with a seriousness I hadn't seen in him before.

"Billy, you coming?"

"Yeah," Billy said, shoving his hands in his pockets as he turned to join us. "I'm right behind you."

1986

PART 4: THE THING THAT SHOULD NOT BE

SURE ENOUGH, BILLY'S PROGNOSTICATION HAD been spot on the money. It hadn't been five minutes when, as silent as a ghost, an evening mist rolled into the Glen Forest valley, blanketing everything with a thick white haze.

A white sheet had settled over the forest and, inconveniently enough, cut off all sight of Fort Liberty. In other words, we'd lost our bearings and walked around the forest as blind as a pack of mole rats.

"I think it's this way," Paul whispered.

"No, you idiot," Jimmy countered, "we already circled back that way. It's this way. Trust me."

The two shot each other with incensed looks and

then turned to Billy to give him the final say.

"You know these woods better than anybody, Billy. Heck, it's in your very name. You and your brother used to go hunting all around these parts. So, tell us, which way is it?" I asked. If anyone could get us out of this scrape, it would be Billy.

After a long contemplative pause, Billy scanned all our faces and said, "I'm not sure."

To say we were disappointed would be the understatement of the year.

"Need I remind you," Paul said, looking over the tops of his rims at Billy, "There's a monster out there somewhere that probably has our scent by now. And if not, it certainly will soon enough."

The silence was broken by the rattle of Mitch shaking his inhaler, and then he sucked it in, held it, and finally exhaled. "I knew it. I just knew it," he said, his voice wavering uncertainly. "We're all gonna die out here."

"Nobody is going to die out here," I replied. The truth was, however, I had no clue what the evening might bring. All I knew was that entertaining negative thoughts would only bog us down. Now wasn't the time to throw ourselves any pity parties. What we needed to do at a time like this was keep our heads up and keep moving.

"What is it, Billy?" Mitch asked, noticing Billy's eyes light up as a lightbulb went off in his head. Not wasting time, Billy drew out his flashlight and flicked on the switch. Its bright beam caused all of us to divert our eyes.

Flashing it on and off, he pointed it at a tree. He repeated the process, turning it on only long enough to make out a tree and then flicking it off again.

"What the hell are you doing?" Jimmy asked, his voice strained through a clenched jaw. "There's a light-hating alien out there," he continued, his hand flying up as he pointed at the woods, "that's probably hunting us as we speak, and you're flashing that thing around as if you're trying to signal it."

"We are going to die out here," Mitch repeated, taking another hit of his inhaler. "I just know it."

"Don't be such a big pussy," Melody said, shooting Mitch the most uncompromising twelve-year-old girl glare any of us had ever seen. He gave her a double take, obviously deflated by a little girl calling him out on his spinelessness. As her reproachful gaze drilled into him, he folded his arms and turned his back to her to better wallow in his gloom.

"I'm looking for markers," Billy informed us, answering Jimmy's previous question. "Marv thought it would be a good idea to spray paint red X's on some of the trees, the further out from base camp we were, in case we ever got lost. Find a red X, and you'll find your way back to Fort Liberty."

"Smart," Paul said, pushing up his glasses for the umpteenth time. "But Jimmy still has a point," Paul continued. "All that flashing will draw the glowing light monster to us like a moth to a flame."

I couldn't help but note the pessimistic tone permeating his voice. But someone had to say it because we were all thinking it.

"It's a risk I'm willing to take. Red X's on brown bark are practically impossible to see in the dark. We might wander through the woods all night if we don't risk it. And with that thing out there, the question you have to ask yourselves is, do we find that marker or stay out here… with it?"

"I vote for the marker," Melody said, her soft voice drawing all our attention to her. Smiling at my sister, I placed a hand on her shoulder, and she immediately pulled me into her arms and gave me the biggest hug of my life.

"It'll be alright," I said, kissing the top of her head like Mom always did. "I promise."

"And I promise I won't let anything happen to you," Billy said, still flashing his light on the nearby trees as he probed the woods. Just then, his beam caught something as it moved across an entire row of tree trunks, and Mitch shrieked like a girl deathly afraid of spiders.

"You saw that, right? It wasn't just me. We all saw it, right?"

Very calmly, Paul reached over and smothered Mitch's mouth with his hand. Paul hushed Mitch, putting a finger to his lips, and everyone fell silent.

We all froze and turned to see what Billy's flashlight had settled on. Standing in the clearing, a couple of dark, sunken eyes with bleeding mascara peered back at us. Even though every single one of us was scared stiff, to our relief, it wasn't a monster but a girl—a high school girl. She wore a cheerleader uniform with gold and royal blue, accompanied by white piping.

Sarah Lewis, captain of the high school cheer squad, stood in the clearing, her clothes torn and stained with blood. Scratches marked her legs and arms, and she was panting heavily as if she'd been running through the woods all night. She raised her hand to shield her eyes and said, "Do you mind?"

"Oh, right. Sorry," Billy replied, lowering his flashlight.

"God," Mitch said, taking another puff on his inhaler, "she scared the living bejesus out of me."

"Sarah?" I asked, turning on my light and shining it at her. "Sarah Lewis?" I then pointed the light at my own face and said, "It's me. Travis. Travis Mahoney."

Sarah shook her head, as if to say "No," and groaned as she cradled her abdomen, which was bleeding profusely. "You kids shouldn't be out here," she murmured, her words filled with fear and pain. "It's not safe. There's a…"

Before she could finish her sentence, she slumped over and, passing out, collapsed to the ground.

Sarah's body fell to the side, and she rolled onto her back, revealing a nasty gash that ran from her hip to the center of her chest. Her shirt was barely hanging together by a thread, but it held, to the disappointment of Mitch, Jimmy, and Paul.

As we stood around her unconscious body,

staring down at her, Jimmy slowly reached down and extended his finger. Inches above her left boob, Billy reached out and slapped his hand away.

"Have some respect," he snapped.

Jimmy just laughed and replied, "What? It's not like we weren't all thinking it."

"Is she dead?" Mitch asked.

Billy knelt down and, touching her neck, checked for a pulse. "She is alive. But just barely."

None of us knew that much about Sarah. Not really, anyway. We all knew the usual stuff that everyone in town knew. We knew that she was the homecoming queen and the class president at Woodridge High. We knew she was the varsity volleyball captain and that, according to Mitch's older sister, Sarah was barely passing her courses.

Additionally, she had babysat Mel and me a few times throughout our lives, but we never talked or did anything other than watch movies and make popcorn before bed. That was about it, though, because none of us knew Sarah—not the real Sarah, anyway. And if it wasn't newsworthy enough to get in our local newspaper, it was probably just gossip from the rumor mill.

It was doubtful that any of us had ever even held a conversation with her, except maybe for Mitch, who only briefly talked to her when she had spent the night at his house once for a slumber party hosted by his sister, Megan.

Sarah moaned, still in pain, and Billy and I ran up to her to see what we could do to help. I sat her up and propped her against the tree as Billy steadied her, preventing her from toppling over again. Although I tried not to look, I couldn't help but steal a glance at her wound. It was bad, but at least no guts were spilling out.

"It'll be okay," Billy said, reassuring Sarah that she would be all right. "I promise."

A collective sigh made its way through the group when he looked over his shoulder at us and added, "Look, you guys, I'm not going to sugarcoat this, but she's lost a lot of blood. She needs disinfectant and stitches. I've got a first aid kit back at Fort Liberty, which we can use. So, help me pick her up."

"Pick her up?" Paul inquired, brushing his glasses back up his nose. "How do you expect us to do that? We're fourteen and barely eighty pounds when wet and fully clothed. She's at least sixteen going on seventeen and is a hundred and twenty pounds of lean, mean, teen-girl muscle."

"Here," Mitch said, drawing out a canteen full of water. "Give her this. It'll help rejuvenate her."

I took it from him and then unscrewed the cap. Putting the mouth of the bottle to her lips, I gently tilted her head up and began to pour. The water drizzled past her claret lips, and she instantly began coughing and hacking. Once she recovered, she looked up at the strange gathering of adolescent faces staring back at her.

"Where am I?" she asked.

"You're in shock," Billy said, touching her shoulder. She looked down at his hand and then up at his brunette mop of hair and smoldering brown eyes.

"I'm still in these goddamn woods, aren't I?"

"I'm afraid so," he answered, his hand lingering on her shoulder.

Sarah then looked at me and grabbed my hand. Then, drawing the canteen to her lips, she drank until nothing was left. Wiping her mouth, she looked at all of our faces again and then tried to get up. She winced in pain as she strained to stand, but all she managed was a grunt before sinking back down and settling into the tree again.

Gripping her side again, she glanced down at her wound and blood-soaked clothes. "Thanks, Trav," she said, her voice still sounding as coarse as cheap sandpaper as she wiped her lips with the back of her hand and gave the canteen back to me.

"No problem," I replied, handing the canteen back to Mitch. I noticed a shiver ripple through Sarah's body, and although the summer days were hot, the Illinois nights could still give you a chill. I took off my jacket and placed it over her shoulders, and she smiled at me and squeezed my arm in gratitude. I nearly melted into a gooey puddle.

"We've got a proper first-aid kit back at Fort Liberty. We can bandage and clean your wounds when we get there."

"For Liberty?" she asked, not recognizing the name.

"It's the name of their stupid tree fort," Mel said, rolling her eyes.

At that very moment, Sarah looked at Mel and grew excited. "Holy shit," Sarah gasped. "Mel, is that you?"

"Yeah," Mel said, fidgeting with her yellow fanny

pack and swaying nervously as she shot Sarah a bashful look.

"You've grown like a weed since I saw you last. Amazing. It feels like I haven't seen you in ages. You're all grown up now."

Mel smiled at the compliment. I'm sure she liked to think of herself as more mature than she actually was, and Sarah's acknowledgment of her made her day.

"I hate to be the bearer of bad news," Billy interrupted, breaking up the small reunion, "but there's a creature out here in these very woods likely to be stalking us as we speak."

We all nodded, but before heading out, he turned his gaze back to Sarah's and asked, "Before we go, though, what can you tell us about what happened? Any little detail might help."

"It was… I don't know how to explain it," Sarah began. She clutched my jacket close to her chest as if something had chilled her to her bones before shaking it off with a shiver and continuing with her story.

"It was awful. I was with Dean, my boyfriend, when it attacked us. We were in the middle of… well, that's not important… anyway, we were interrupted by the screams, and we stopped to see what was going on."

Jimmy leaned over to Paul and, raising his hand to his mouth, whispered, "She's talking about s-e-x."

"I know," Paul whispered back. I shot them a harsh glance and shook my head, letting them know this wasn't the time for joking around.

"At first, nothing made sense," Sarah continued. "It was utter chaos and, to be honest, it felt like someone was pranking us. Like a senior prank or something. We got out of the Firebird to see what the commotion was about, and before I knew it..." she paused, wiping a tear from her cheek as she struggled to recall the horrific events.

"It's all right," I said, touching her shoulder. She smiled at me, sniffled, and wiped a tear from the corner of her eye.

"Dean turned to me, taking my hands in his, and said, 'Everything will be alright.' He was about to say something more when, out of the blue, something burst through his chest and yanked him out of my arms. His body flew up into the trees and... just like that, he was gone. The next thing I know, there's a bone-shattering crunch, and his blood splatters everywhere. It got in my eyes. In my mouth, even. All I could do was stand there in shock, looking down at the blood on my clothes and hands."

"Gross," Melody whispered. I shot her a curt glance, which only elicited a shrug from her.

"I know it's difficult right now," Billy spoke, his voice smooth and reassuring. "But what did this do to you?"

"They look like claw marks," Mitch said. Paul adjusted his glasses and nodded in agreement while Jimmy picked a booger out of his nose and flicked it to the ground.

"I don't know. In the chaos of it all, I didn't get a good look at it. But it was big. And it had a strange aura to it. It glowed a bluish-purple, like a black light. Luminous. That's the word. It had nine tails, and they had what appeared to be feathers on their tips. But they weren't feathers. They were more like razor blades."

Mitch gulped. "Tails with razor blades? That doesn't sound good."

Sarah cleared her throat. "I was frozen with fear, unable to force my feet to move, and then, I felt this sharp, lacerating sting bite into my stomach. One of the feather-tipped tails had brushed up against me. A pain like nothing I'd ever experienced before surged through my entire body, and it felt as though all of my nerves were on fire. I wanted to scream so badly, but I couldn't. The pain was so great that all I could do was gasp silently… hoping, praying, that I'd just die."

"Then what happened?" asked Paul, pushing his glasses up. Like all of us, he was engrossed in her story. The story of how she managed to survive her brush with death.

"I must have passed out from the pain. The next thing I know, I'm waking up beneath someone's Jeep, no trace of the monster."

She wiped another tear from her cheek, her mascara running down her face, and then threw her arm over Billy and me. We helped Sarah to her feet, and she grunted as she got fully up for the first time since we'd found her standing in the middle of the woods.

My jacket slipped from her grasp and fluttered to the ground. I snatched it up and offered it to her, but she just raised her hand and gestured for me to keep it.

A sharp twinge of pain overcame her, and Sarah

clutched her waist and groaned.

"That wound is pretty bad," I said. Maybe we should tie it off first. Does anybody have anything?" I turned to the boys, who looked at one another and back to me. Nothing.

"Wait," Melody said, her fingers rummaging through her fanny pack as she searched for something. Finding what she was looking for, she quickly drew out one of Mom's oversized floral head scarves.

Instantly, I recognized it from old photos of Mom as a college kid in the '60s and '70s. All her clothes seemed to consist of tie-dye shirts, bell-bottom jeans, and brightly colored headscarves. I'll never know how it ended up in Melody's fanny pack, but my sister seemed to be quite the pack rat.

"You can use this."

"Perfect," Sarah murmured, taking it from Mel. She quickly wrapped herself up, tying off the knot with a grunt, then looked back up at Melody and thanked her. "You're a lifesaver, kiddo."

"We girls have to stick together," Mel said, "because these idiots are completely useless."

Unable to resist smiling, Sarah scanned our faces and stepped forward with another pain-laced grunt.

"You kids have a treehouse somewhere near here, right? You mentioned it earlier. What was the name, again? Oh, right. For Liberty. Right, Billy? Marvin told me how he'd built it with his kid brother."

Billy nodded. "You knew my brother?"

Sarah smiled at him, which confirmed what we already expected her answer to be. "He was a grade above me," she continued, "But we all hung out in the same crew. So, yeah, Marv and I were as thick as thieves."

Billy nodded, a subtle smile forming as he recalled the fond memories of building Fort Liberty with his brother. "We built it with our dad," he informed her, his voice growing quiet. "I was only one when our dad shipped off to Saigon. Marv was six. But Dad never came back from the war. I don't know. All I can remember of that day, the day we all found out, was a military officer with a flag arriving on our doorstep. He handed it to my mom, who stood there in shock, unable to say anything. She went completely numb, you know? And that was that."

"I'm sorry," Sarah said, softly touching Billy's shoulder. "I didn't know. I mean, Marvin never talked about your dad."

"Sorry, man," Mitch said, giving his condolences.

"Yeah, sorry, man," Paul added, "that sucks."

"I never knew my old man, either," Jimmy said. "He got locked up before I was out of diapers. My mom calls him a two-timing, no-good, lying scumbag. I don't know what I'm trying to say. I guess, at least, your dad died a hero. That's not nothing, man."

"Hey, Billy," I said, "Father or no, at least yours loved you. He spent time with you guys out here. He taught your brother survival skills, and then Marv taught you." I turned and gestured to the wilderness all around us. "That has to count for something. Besides," I added, turning back to Billy, "he gave us all Fort Liberty. And for that, we're all eternally grateful."

"Here, here!" Paul sounded off. We all followed suit with a more robust *"Here, here."*

"Thanks," Billy replied, wiping a tear from the corner of his eye with his thumb. "I appreciate that."

It was clear to me that Billy was opening up to us now because he felt this might be his last opportunity. I didn't like the implications of that, so I shook the thought from my mind and focused on the task at hand. Getting back to Fort Liberty.

"Hey, kiddo," I said, turning to Melody. "What

else do you have in that fanny pack that we might be able to use to help us get back to base?"

"X marks the spot," Melody said.

"What?" I asked. The full weight of her words not yet registering in my mind.

"Wait, what did you say?" Billy asked, spinning around as he looked at Melody with large, excited eyes.

Sarah followed our gazes, and Melody pointed above our heads. All of us followed the direction of her little finger and looked up to find the marker on the tree. "Over there!"

We all let out a collective sigh of relief, and Mitch wheezed, "We're saved," before taking another hit of his inhaler.

But Mitch spoke too soon because, at that moment, a horrifying beastly cry rose from the darkness. The creature was near. Its howling roar was so loud it shook the trees all around us, and I knew it was only mere feet away from our position.

Strangely enough, I'd heard a similar cry before. I'd once listened to a baboon's roar at the zoo, and it was so loud that it left my ears ringing for the better part of the day. You don't expect a baboon to sound like Death gargling Pop Rocks at ninety-six decibels, but they do.

Still, this creature… this alien… was much, much worse. Its cry not only split our ears open so they bled, but it filled us from head to toe with abject terror.

Worse than its hideous roar, though, was what we saw when we turned in the direction the sound had come from. That dreaded blue-violet glow was cutting through the trees and headed straight toward us.

"Run!" I whispered as loudly as I dared without my voice growing above a soft murmur.

Paul, Mitch, and Billy swiftly ran up the trail leading to the treehouse. Turning to follow them, I glimpsed Melody, frozen with fear, out of the corner of my eye. I reached out to grab her hand, but Sarah appeared as if out of nowhere and beat me to it.

Sarah, Mel, and I ran side-by-side as we raced after the others. I glanced back at the worst possible time and saw the hideous beast just as the fog lifted. Its horrifying look defied description.

I gulped hard, tugging on my shirt collar as I continued up the trail. In the distance, the yellow kerosene glow of Fort Liberty lit up much of the surrounding area, a beacon guiding us home. But we weren't the only ones who could see it. The creature, still sensitive to light, also took notice and emitted an angry, guttural growl that caused Mel to flinch and cover her ears as she ran.

Sarah shot me a worried look, but I could do nothing. That's when, to everyone's astonishment, Mitch skidded to a stop in the middle of the trail. He began patting himself down, searching his pockets for something.

"What are you doing?" asked Paul.

"I have a Butterfinger somewhere on me." Fishing out the candy bar, he smiled and held it up.

Jimmy jumped up and quickly snatched it from his hand, "Give it here, you cock-sucker." He ripped the wrapper open and, lobbing it like a grenade, threw the candy bar twenty feet behind us. It landed about five feet in front of the monster.

"Come on, come on!" Paul said, anxiously hopping up and down as he waved everyone to continue up the path. "That will only distract it for so long. We've got to move, people."

"Yeah," Jimmy said, shoving Mitch aside as he raced past everyone. "Last one to Fort Liberty is a butt-munch!"

Sarah and Mel joined Paul and the others when Mel glanced back in time to see the creature walk up to the candy bar and begin sniffing it. Sarah also looked back, but startled by what she saw—remembering the terrible massacre at Make-Out Point—she gripped Mel tightly by her sleeve and tugged even harder. "Don't stop," she said. "We're almost there."

Once again, Billy and I found ourselves standing beside one another. Both of us watched the alien sniff and paw at the candy bar. It opened its long snout and licked at the Butterfinger lying in the dirt. When it realized it was edible, it snarfed it down.

After licking its chops, the alien craned its neck and looked up at the moon. Then, it made a strange cry that sounded like a mix between a goose honking and a dog barking. This caterwauling continued until cloud cover rolled in, blotting out the moon. As the sky dimmed, the beast's yowling subsided. At the same time, however, its mysterious bluish-purple glow intensified, and then it looked right at us.

Billy looked at me and said, "Come on. We'd better catch up with the others."

I nodded, and we turned and followed after everyone. At the same time, I couldn't help but feel relief since Fort Liberty sat at the crest of the hill, its twinkling Christmas lights and kerosene lamps, like enormous fireflies, guiding us home.

5

1986
PART 5: THE PLAN

WINDED AND DRENCHED IN SWEAT, WE returned to Fort Liberty in record time. How we navigated the dark terrain with a glowing monster on our trail and still managed not to lose anyone was beyond me. Scurrying up the rope ladder, we climbed into the treehouse, snuffed the kerosene lamps, unplugged the twinkle lights to conserve batteries, drew up the rope ladder, latched all the windows, and threw a two-by-four bracer across the door.

None of us were sure it would keep the monster at bay, but it was better than nothing.

"No lights," Sarah whispered, taking our flashlights and tossing them into a pile on the nearest sleeping bag. "It doesn't like light. Of that much, I'm certain. From here on out, we navigate by moonlight."

"I don't get it," Melody said. "Why doesn't it like

light?"

"I bet it has something to do with the infrared spectrum," Paul interjected, sharing his scientific theory with the group.

"Oh, great. Here comes another theory from 'The Brain'," Jimmy said, throwing his arms on his hips and rolling his eyes.

"That's right. I have a theory," Paul said in erudite fashion, pushing up his glasses for added effect. Jimmy's eyes widened as he looked at all of us as if to say, *See, I told you so.* "That thing out there... our light seems to royally tick it off. I asked myself why, and then I thought, what if what Sarah saw was accurate, and this thing, presumably, does emit ultraviolet light. Well, that's the opposite kind of light to our own, right? So—"

"So, what are you saying? Our light hurts it?" Mitch asked, cutting into Paul's explanation.

"More like irritates the hell out of it. Look at those cars, the creature batted them around as if they were Matchbox toys." Paul scanned our faces and then sighed. "Of course, it's just a theory. After all, that thing is a never-before-cataloged form of extraterrestrial life, so it might just be generally pissy."

"The Smart Dweeb here is onto something," Jimmy said. "It seems to prefer the ultraviolet light. Warm light, like our flashlights, only gives it burns and royally pisses it off."

"I just said that," Paul noted, pushing his glasses up again. Jimmy merely ignored him before continuing on.

"But how can we use that to our advantage?"

"We don't," Billy replied. "Not exactly, anyway. If what both of you are saying is true, we'll hole up here for the night. Then, tomorrow, after sunup, that thing will be forced to hide if it doesn't want to burn up. If it doesn't like our flashlights, then it will hate the scorching daylight. If and when it hides from the sun, then we're home free, and we run like Hell back to town. Back to my house."

Sarah looked at Billy and asked, "What if it's still out there after sunrise?"

"Then we'll know we were wrong," I said, scanning everyone's anxious faces. "And then we will have to come up with a new plan. But one thing at a time. First, we focus on getting through the night."

"Assuming we can make it through the night," Melody said, "I mean, where will we even go to the toilet at?"

"Do you have to go?" I asked. She nodded.

"Over here," Billy said, showing her to a side curtain, which was just a blue tarp strung up over an old shower pole that Marv had bolted to the wall. Drawing back the tarp, her face grew dour when she saw little more than a large bucket with a toilet seat fastened onto it.

"You've got to be kidding me," Melody said, eyeing it skeptically. "I can't use that."

"That's all we have, I'm afraid," Billy said apologetically.

Melody shook her head in protest and folded her arms across her chest. "I can't go in that. Not with everyone watching me."

"That's what the curtain is for," Mitch said.

She adamantly shook her head as if to say, "Nuh-uh...

no freaking way."

"Who's being a big fat pussy, now?" Mitch asked, as he goaded Mel, a large grin forming on his face as he finally got back for all her earlier insults.

This seemed to do the trick because whether she was motivated not to let him get the best of her, or just pissed off, she exhaled dramatically and mumbled, "Fine."

Drawing the curtain shut behind her, we shared awkward glances when a tiny drizzle started. Unable to help himself, Jimmy began to snigger.

"Hey, shut your trap, you little shit-head," Sarah scolded, shooting Jimmy an icy death glare. "And one more thing, you little prick, you glance down at my chest one more time, and I'll take this blade and cut your balls off with it."

She drew out Jimmy's switchblade and flipped it around expertly. Locking the blade in place, she tapped it against his inner thigh, causing him to gulp nervously.

Jimmy raised his hands in surrender and whispered tersely from the corner of his mouth, "Sorry. My bad."

"Hey, did she pick-pocket you?" Paul asked. "I didn't even see her do it."

Jimmy shrugged. He had no clue how she managed that little trick.

How a nice midwestern girl like her knew how to wield a switchblade was beyond me, but Sarah was determined to keep everyone safe, so it was probably better if she held onto it anyway.

"Can I have my knife back now?" Jimmy asked. Sarah flipped it around again, folded it up, and then slid it into her cheerleader skirt's waistband, since it didn't exactly have any pockets.

"No," she replied.

Jimmy folded his arms and stomped over to the corner of the treehouse to pout, mad that he lost his prized possession.

Without warning, Sarah winced as a surge of pain rushed through her. Groaning, she clutched her abdomen and sat down on the bench seat along the side wall.

"What's the matter?" I asked.

"I think my adrenaline is wearing off and my body is finally realizing how beat up it is."

"Hang on," Billy said, rushing to the bench where Sarah sat. Wasting no time, Billy opened the second half of the bench, which opened like a secret treasure chest, and hastily retrieved the first aid kit. He set it down on the bench beside Sarah, opened it, and rummaged through its contents until he found a bottle of Bactine, a roll of gauze, some thread, and a sewing needle. "We need to get you stitched up and disinfect that wound before it festers."

Sarah took the supplies and sat them on her lap. She scanned our faces and said, "Look, I need help with this. If I pass out from the pain, I'll need someone who knows how to sew to stitch me up." After a long silence, she asked, "Can any of you sew? Anybody? Nobody?"

When no one answered her question, she let out an abrupt sigh and said, "Just my luck."

"We're middle schoolers," Paul said, pushing up his glasses. "We haven't learned that stuff yet."

"I'll do it," a voice said, rising to the occasion. The blue privacy curtain drew back, and Melody stood looking right as rain. "I sew new clothes for my dolls all the time. I can do it."

"You sure?" Sarah asked, eyeing the twelve-year-old standing before her. "It'll be a little gross and scary."

"You've obviously never seen my brother eat, have you?"

This caused Sarah to laugh for the first time all night. Her laugh immediately triggered a moan, and she clutched her side again, "Don't make me laugh," she said, still smiling.

Her smile was like a ray of sunshine, and for that split second, we all forgot about the terrors lurking outside and basked in her youthful radiance.

"Actually, I have," she chortled. "Point taken."

"Besides, I'm twelve, not a baby. You were probably smoking cigarettes and having sex at twelve," Melody said, teasing Sarah.

Sarah laughed again, and another surge of pain forced her to endure another uncomfortable groan.

"Right. My comedian sister will handle it," I said, looking at Sarah. She nodded at me, and Mel got on her knees, threaded the needle from the first-aid kit, and slowly pushed the sharp point into Sarah's skin.

"Fudge-dick!" she screamed, cursing to help combat the excruciating pain.

"Fudge-dick?" Mitch asked, looking around at us. But we had no clue and merely shook our heads.

"It's okay," Melody said, looking up into Sarah's eyes. "You can say the 'F-word' if you want. I mean, we've all heard it before."

"Thanks," Sarah replied. "I appreciate that. But I was talking about him." She tilted her head at Jimmy, who spun around and looked at all of us with a dopey, shocked expression on his face.

"Why me? Why am I the fudge dick?"

"She's just messing with you," I said, looking over at Sarah. She nodded and winced again as my kid sister pushed the needle and thread into her abdomen.

As the needle punctured her skin a second time, drawing the tiniest thimble of blood, Paul's eyes rolled back in his head, his body went limp, and he fainted right in the center of the treehouse. He hit the floor with a thump, and we all looked down at him.

"If anyone is a fudge-dick," Jimmy mumbled, still sore about being singled out, "it's this dillweed here."

Mitch, Paul's best friend in the whole world, knelt beside him and began shaking his shoulder. "Hey, Paul. You all right?"

Paul slowly sat up, with Mitch's help, and pushed his glasses back up. He asked, "What happened?"

"You fainted."

"No, I didn't," Paul said, standing back up. When he looked over again at Mel sewing up Sarah's wound, he instantly passed out again.

Mitch was about to try to help him up when Billy raised a hand. "It's probably better if you just leave him be. Let him sleep through it." Mitch nodded, and we all turned and watched my little sister do something none of us had the guts to do. Push a needle through someone's bloody wound and stitch up their skin. Apparently, all her sewing for her dolls paid off, and I couldn't have been prouder of my little sis than at this moment.

Pacing back and forth, I finally turned to Billy, who met my gaze at the same time. "So, what now?" we said, each of us speaking the same thought simultaneously.

At that precise moment, Paul's eyes opened and he mumbled, "What'd I miss?"

Mitch helped him sit up just as Melody finished stitching Sarah up. "Nothing much," Mitch replied, rubbing Paul's back.

"Right. This is what we need to do," Billy began, as he relayed the orders. "Paul, you get on the walkies and call for help. Try every frequency if you have to, but you get somebody on the horn and bring them up to speed. Jimmy and Mitch, I need you both to take that rope hanging on the wall and string up these blankets as curtains. Mitch, you take those infrared hunting binoculars from Marv's tote over in the corner and keep an eye out for that creature."

Finally, Billy turned to me and said, "Trav, I need

you to take a count of our rations, portion them off for each person here, and see if there's anything else we might be able to use for our defense. Boys, tonight we make a stand. Tonight, we protect Fort Liberty with everything we've got."

"What will you do?" asked Paul.

Billy went over to the wall and opened a small closet. Inside was Marv's old shotgun and a box of buckshot. Drawing it out, he cracked the barrel and began loading the shells. "I have Marv's old scattergun. He usually used it to shoot down quail and small game. He even killed a badger or two. And there was this one time he used it to scare off a bear. If it worked for a bear, I'm willing to bet it'll work for that thing out there, too."

"I hate to break it to you," Jimmy said. "But that ain't no bear out there. It's, like, ten times worse and probably much meaner—razor blades for tails, remember?"

"Guys," Mitch said, his voice trembling as severely as the binoculars in his hands. "It's directly below us." He nodded at the wood floor as if to say, *It's right there.*

Sure enough, indigo light began seeping through

the cracks in the floor, and everyone grew so silent you could hear a mosquito fart.

Billy merely raised his hand as though he were an orchestral conductor bringing everything to a standstill before the big crescendo and gestured for everyone to hush.

"Don't do it," Paul whispered, recognizing that look in Billy's eyes. "Please, Billy. It's not worth dying for."

"You don't understand," Billy said, his voice low and steady. "Fort Liberty is all I have left of him. And I'd die a thousand times to keep that last part of him. If I can keep you all safe, too, that's just a bonus."

Billy cocked the shotgun and looked at us all one last time. "Whatever you do, don't come out here. Understand? If I see any of your ugly mugs out here, I'm aiming this scattergun at your balls. You hear me?"

We all nodded, a somberness coming over us. With that, Billy unlatched the front door and slid the bracer beam out of its slot. Reaching down, he gripped the handle and opened the door. Unexpectedly, Sarah's voice cut through all the tension and uncertainty and said, "Wait."

Billy turned, and she strode up to him with a tilt

and sway to her hips like nothing we'd ever seen before. Bending down, she took his face in her palms and kissed him smack dab on his lips. We watched it unfold like a romantic scene from the movie *Endless Love,* and all stood there grinning like village idiots.

Sarah Lewis was the closest thing to a real woman we knew who wasn't one of our mothers. She had kissed him, and she'd kissed him long and good. She may have even slipped him some tongue. And for that, Billy would go down as a legend in our book.

"What was that for?" Billy asked, half beside himself, still wrapped up in her embrace.

"For saving my life," she informed, smiling down at him. "And for being the bravest kid I've ever met. And that's a fact." She reached up, rubbed some lipstick off his lips with her thumb, and then smiled at him. Billy blushed.

"Don't worry." I gently touched Melody's elbow to console her now that her first crush was taken. "Someday, your Prince Charming will come. Maybe not today. Maybe not tomorrow… but he'll come."

"Don't be a dickhead," she said, wiping a tear from her cheek. "I'm not crying because Billy likes Sarah more than me. I'm crying because he's leaving us to die out there."

Even though I knew that she harbored feelings for Billy, she wasn't wrong. Billy would die if he faced that thing alone.

Billy gave us all one final glance, then stepped outside, his shotgun aimed squarely in front of him, just as his brother had taught him.

Once the door shut behind him, we stood in a moment of silence. Then, with bated breath, we turned to one another and strained our ears to try to hear what was happening.

Blam!

The sound of the shotgun going off startled us all. But more shocking, perhaps, was when Billy started shouting, "Get out of here!" at the top of his lungs. *Blam!* Another blast. "Git, I said!"

"How many shells did he take with him?" Paul asked.

"A handful," Mitch replied.

Another blast followed by another had us rattled.

Then nothing. Everything drew quiet and we waited with bated breath.

After a lengthy silence, Billy's voice came through the wall, and a wave of relief washed over us. Even

Sarah let out a sigh. "I think I scared it off. I'm going to climb down to take a closer look," he informed us.

"No!" I shouted and raced toward the door. Jimmy body-checked me into the wall, and Mitch and Paul leaped onto me and held me down.

"I can't let you go out there," Jimmy growled. "You heard what Billy said. Nobody goes out there for nothing. We die if we go out there, man."

"For anything," Paul corrected, pushing his black-rimmed eyeglasses up the bridge of his nose.

"Really?" Jimmy asked, shooting him a sideways glance. "Is this the time you want to start with me, Four-Eyes?"

"Jeez, Mad Dog, I didn't think you'd get so mad."

"Shut up," Jimmy shouted, lunging at Paul. "You know I hate that stupid nickname!"

Mitch and I grabbed Jimmy by the underarms just in time to stop him from hitting Paul across the face, and, to our surprise, Paul simply snickered, pushed his glasses up, and muttered, "Can't see why. It's so fitting."

"What'd you say?" Jimmy said, shaking us off. "Why don't you say that to my face?"

Paul merely shrugged and looked away rather

than stoke the flames of Jimmy's ire any further. Jimmy had always had a hot temper, but it was exasperated by everything we'd been through tonight.

Unexpectedly, Melody strode over and kicked Jimmy in the balls as hard as she could. Jimmy collapsed to the floor and, tears streaming from the corners of his eyes, he wheezed, "What'd you go and do that for?"

"You're being a butt-head, and Billy needs our help. I don't care what anyone says, but we're going to help him."

"Right," Sarah agreed, backing up my little sis. "Melody is right. We're in this together."

Finally, everyone being on the same page, I walked over to the wall and grabbed the hatchet from it. Holding it out as a warning to anyone who dared come near, I said, "I don't care what Billy said or what anyone else might say. That's my best friend out there, and I, for one, ain't going to sit on my thumbs doing nothing. My only question is, are you guys in or out?"

Everyone in the treehouse shared hushed glances and then nodded. Mitch was the first to speak. "You bet we are."

Sarah put her arm around Melody and stood firm.

"Mel is right, Billy is out there and needs our help. Besides, I kind of like the kid, so yeah, you bet your asses we're in."

"What about you, numb-nuts?" I asked, looking down at Jimmy. "You in or out?"

"Jeez, it's not like you give a guy any choice. I'm in," he replied, struggling to his feet.

"All right, then. Let's do this."

6

1986
PART 6: FIGHTING FIRE WITH FIRE

With that out of the way, we had our plan. It may not have been the best thought-out plan, but we weren't military strategists. We were a bunch of kids from Woodridge, trapped in the woods with a freaking alien monster. It's the best we could come up with given the circumstances.

I went over to the back bench, which ran the length of the back wall, and lifted the seat. I drew out the reserve canister of kerosene and looked over my shoulder at everyone.

"Listen," I said, breaking the silence. "I don't know what this night will bring, but you all do what you've gotta do to survive. I won't hold it against you if you stay behind and batten down the hatches. But these are our woods, this is our time, and that thing out there picked the wrong night to mess with the Lords of Summer. This is mother-fracking Fort Liberty, for Christ's sake! And I, for one, sure as hell intend to defend it."

Rising to my feet, the tin of kerosene in one hand, my hatchet in the other, I turned toward the door and inhaled deeply. However, to my surprise, Sarah appeared in front of me before I could step out, blocking my path.

Her hands were on her hips, and she shot me a stern look. "I just need to know one thing, Travis. Are you sure you know what you're doing?"

"I'm sure," I replied.

Sarah cocked her head and narrowed her eyes at me as though she were scanning my innermost thoughts to see if they were sincere. Then, reaching into her pocket, she pulled out something metallic and tossed it to me. "In that case, you'll need this."

I caught it, nearly dropping the hatchet as I fumbled to clasp onto everything, and looked down at the stainless steel Zippo lighter resting in my hands.

"A lighter?" I asked.

"It was Dean's," she said. "He smoked."

I looked her in the eyes, and she stepped aside, letting me pass. We both nodded at one another, knowing there was nothing left to say. As I walked past her, Sarah leaned over to Melody and said, "Your brother has some giant flippin' balls on him, I'll give him that much."

Sarah whipped out the switchblade with a proficiency that was equally scary and sexy, and locked the blade into place. "Well, shit," she said, her blue eyes locking with mine. "Your mom would kill me if I ever let anything happen to you. I'd rather take my chances with that thing out there than have to face her wrath."

Melody marched across the inside of the treehouse, shoving Jimmy and Mitch aside as she cut through us. Then, raising her slender leg, she kicked open the treehouse door like the badass she was and strode out onto the balcony. Looking over her shoulder, she narrowed her eyes at us and asked, "Well, you blanket-clutching, thumb-sucking sissies coming or what?"

"Jeez, your sister is scary," Paul said.

"Tell me about it," Mitch said, speaking from experience.

Once we joined Melody on the deck, I looked back at the whole gang. They nodded, expressing their unspoken support for the mission. None of us were giving up. We were a brotherhood. And this summer belonged to us. Not to them—not to some stinking alien from another world.

"Does anybody have eyes on him?" I asked as we all took up different positions on the balcony.

"Over there," cried Melody. We all ran to her location in time to see the creature drag Billy over the hill roughly fifty meters away.

"It's got him," I shouted. "It's taken Billy!"

We clamored down the treehouse rope as fast as possible, dropping to the ground and scanning our immediate surroundings for any additional signs of danger. Once we knew the area was secure, Paul picked up the shovel, I handed Mitch my hatchet while I opted to keep the lighter and kerosene, and Jimmy grabbed a green duffel bag with "Top Secret" written on it in black Sharpie.

As curious as the bag was, none of us had time to investigate its contents. We had to save Billy.

When we reached the top of the hill to rescue Billy, we found the creature straddling him. Its razor-toothed, gaping maw dripped with blue, glowing slime, and its tongue lathered Billy's face with alien mucus. The beast snapped its jaws and let loose a resonant growl. Billy yelped and threw his hands up in front of his face, but it seemed the creature was testing him.

Fort Liberty's lights lit up to full, its glow flooding into the night and seeping into the cracks of the surrounding trees. We looked back to see yellow, green, and red smoke rising behind us as Jimmy trudged up the hill, a broad grin on his face. He wore a red headband *à la* John Rambo and had a bandolier of Black Cat firecrackers strapped across his chest. As the smoke filled the woods, he reached into his duffel bag and pulled out two reloadable mortars.

"This thing doesn't like light," he said, his grin spreading to manic proportions. "Well, I say we light up this whole damn forest! This thing drew first blood, and we sure as hell are gonna draw last blood."

"Fireworks?" Mitch and Paul asked simultaneously as they leaned over to look at what else Jimmy had in his bag. Jimmy brought his entire reserve, which he'd been saving up. It was clear he wasn't playing any more games. This was the real deal.

This was war.

"Everything I've saved for the past two summers," Jimmy said, pulling out several medium-sized bottle rockets, a few Roman candles, and more Black Cats.

He began handing off fireworks to everyone, saving the best and baddest for Melody. Eight-inch mortars with six rounds of giant starbursts each—twelve rounds in total. He placed it into her hand and said, "Just aim it and shoot. And for what it's worth, I'm sorry for being such a dick."

"Apology accepted," Melody said, her eyes sparkling with excitement as she held the mortar tubes in her hands.

"Still got that lighter?" Jimmy asked, his gaze turning to me. I nodded and flipped the lid. Armed with fireworks, we all turned toward the creature, eyeing us with caution from its six eyes, and I shouted, "Hey, you ugly turd-face! Hope you brought your intergalactic sunscreen because you're about to get roasted!"

The creature looked up at us and shifted its stance—unsure whether it should fight or flee. We were much smaller than it, but it was outnumbered seven to one. Sure, we were simply prey, by its estimation. But we were united. And this gave it pause.

The faint rattle of cans being shaken could be heard, and emerging from the group was my little sister, Mel, holding two canisters of Mom's finest hairspray in each hand. "Light 'em up, boys!"

I flicked the flint of the Zippo lighter, and the flame leaped from the wick and flashed hot orange. Holding up the lighter, Melody and I glanced at each other in mutual recognition, and she mashed down on the plastic tabs.

Flames leaped out as the aerosol hairspray caught fire, and, letting forth the loudest battle cry we could muster, all six of us charged down the hill toward the beast.

Melody pulled out one of the mortars, and like the little psychopath she was, she used her hairspray flamethrower to light the fuse, laughing hysterically as she did so.

The entire gang launched off a steady volley of fireworks as we went. The beast roared and rattled off a ferocious warning, but we weren't deterred. We continued to push it back deeper into the woods. Every once in a while, one of our fireworks would pelt the beast's hide, and it would hiss in fright like a startled cat.

Fireworks zipped and zoomed all about, and then, setting her hairspray down, Melody picked up the second mortar that Jimmy had given her and lit the fuse. "Get away from my friend!" she screamed in that twelve-year-old girl, downright terrifying voice.

BLAM! KA-BLAM! BLAM-BLAM!

Starbursts exploded all around. One of them even pelted the creature in its face. It yelped and skirted back, allowing Billy the wiggle room he needed to scramble back on his hands and feet and make his escape.

BLAM! BLAM!

The creature roared as fiery stars lit up the darkness with brilliant, multi-colored light. I saw my chance and threw the kerosene can into the air. We all watched as it spun as if in slow motion, only for it to land a couple of yards behind the beast.

A bang and a whistle filled the air, and one of Melody's mortars hit the gas pooling out from the can, igniting it. A small explosion erupted behind the beast, and it jumped in fright, whipping its nine glowing tails spastically in the air as flames rose higher and higher behind it. Trapped between a wall of fire and an angry mob of children with boomsticks, the creature snorted and huffed noisily, expressing its displeasure.

The monster circled about skittishly, leaving Billy lying in the dirt, covered in blue, glowing slime. As it paced back and forth like a nervous tiger, its six-eyed snout snapping at the air and letting out gurgles and chirps, it grew increasingly agitated. Maybe the light did hurt it.

BLAM! Another burst was followed by a direct hit! The creature was genuinely spooked now and looked like it had had enough of this nonsense. It glanced at all the shouting faces and slowly backed away, like a cautious alley cat backing away from a pack of snarling junkyard dogs.

Then, Jimmy did the unexpected and, dashing forward, tore the axe out of Mitch's hands as he ran past and charged the alien creature, shouting at the top of his lungs, *"MAD DAWWWG!"*

"Did he just say Mad Dog?" Paul asked as we all turned to watch Jimmy go completely ape-shit on the alien.

As Jimmy charged forward like a raging bull about to pulverize its matador, fireworks went off all around him, and something marvelously unexpected happened. The beast tucked its numerous spiked tails into itself and, realizing it was bested, turned back toward the woods and galloped off, disappearing into the trees. It was a full retreat.

We all cheered as it fled, jumping up and down—hooting and hollering and making sure it remembered our voices.

"Good riddance!" Melody said as she kicked the dirt and shook her fists.

Sarah let out a sigh, feeling weak. She sank to her knees and sat on the ground a couple of meters from us, taking a deep breath and then exhaling slowly. "Well, that was fun… *not*," she said sarcastically.

"Hey," I said, extending my hand toward Billy, who was sitting on the ground, dripping with blue slime. After clearing some goo from his face, Billy looked up and scanned all our grateful faces. "You didn't listen to me."

"I couldn't let you die out here all alone, hero," I said.

"Yeah, what he said," Jimmy retorted, slinging the axe across his shoulders.

Paul and Mitch nodded, and Melody ran up to

Billy, who sat in the dirt, covered in slime, and practically pounced on him, forcing him to catch her as she threw her arms around his neck. He nearly toppled over, barely managing to stay upright as she curled up into his embrace like a baby koala.

"Whoa there, kiddo. It's all right. I'm all right. We're all safe now."

At last, Billy reached up and took my hand. Our eyes met, sharing a brief acknowledgment that we'd made it. I pulled him to his feet with a heave-ho, and Mel slid off. Slathered in goop herself, she wiped some off her chest and flicked it off her fingertips. Then, raising her fingers to her nose, she sniffed her hand, her face turning sour. "It smells like ass," she informed, trying to flick the rest of the slime off but not having any luck.

"Guys," Mitch interjected, "does anyone have the sneaking feeling that this is the calm before the storm? I mean, with that thing still out there, will Woodridge ever be safe?"

As the sun peaked over the horizon, we all shared concerned looks. Mitch had put into words what we had been thinking silently to ourselves. For whatever reason, this didn't feel over. Not by a long shot.

"I can't even begin to think about more aliens right now," Paul said, running his fingers through his curly hair. "I'm still worried about the one we have out there."

"It'll probably find a cave or someplace dark to hide once the sun is fully up. Which means we have time," I said.

"Time…for what?" asked Jimmy.

"Time to prepare ourselves for whatever comes next," Billy answered, drawing up his shotgun. It, too, was covered in slime, but that didn't deter him from striking a pose and looking heroic as all get out.

A clap of thunder startled us all, but it wasn't thunder. It was a sonic boom. We all looked up at the early morning sky to see hundreds of flaming streaks cutting through the atmosphere as a meteor shower rained down all across the horizon, as far as our eyes could see.

"Well, shit," Jimmy said, letting out a drawn-out sigh. "There goes the neighborhood."

We all fell silent as we watched the meteors streaming down from the sky. Bluish-purple dust tails trailed behind them, and they emitted the same kind of glow as the ultraviolet creature. That's how we knew. That's how we knew it was the beginning of the invasion.

"Guys, I don't know about you all, but I have a bad feeling about this," Sarah said, her hands on her hips as she gazed up at the sky. Melody ran up to her and hugged her, tears in her eyes.

"I don't want you to die," Melody squeaked as she broke down into sobs.

"I'm not going anywhere," Sarah informed her. She looked up and scanned all of our faces. "I won't leave you kids alone. I intend to see you home safe, and that's a promise."

The abrupt *cha-shunk* of Billy's shotgun cocking startled us, and our attention flitted back to him. To our shock, though, he was smiling—a white-toothed grin stretching from ear to ear.

"Why are you grinning like that?" Paul asked. "It's creeping me out."

"Because I know something you don't," he said.

"And what's that?" I asked.

"The dawn is breaking, and between my dad and Marvin, I have a whole arsenal back at my house. I'm talking about handguns, rifles, bump stocks, M16s, KA-BAR knives, and even a few grenades left over from my dad's war stash. I'm thinking we head to my house and stock up on ammunition and supplies. Then, we give these alien S.O.B's a proper American welcome and show them why this is the land of the Free and the home of the Brave."

"Damn straight!" Mitch said, pumping his fist.

"More guns are better than none," I agreed.

"They'd certainly be better for fending off alien pests than fireworks," Sarah added. "Count me in."

"Count me in, too," Jimmy said. "I was just getting warmed up, but I can picture a nice alien trophy up on my wall!"

"That's only if your mom lets you keep it on your wall," Paul added.

"Why?" Jimmy asked, shooting Paul a tart look. "Why must you always ruin things?"

"I don't know," Paul replied in a dejected-sounding voice.

Sarah tossed her blond hair over her shoulders and sauntered over to Billy. Slinging her arm across his neck, she leaned in and whispered, "Hey, kid, mind if I use your shower when we get back to your place? I smell like a ripe ole swamp."

Billy gulped and looked back at us, and we all gave

him the thumbs up. He waved us back as if he were shooing us away and then continued with Sarah draped over his shoulder. "Uh, sure," he replied, his voice almost cracking. "I'm sure my mom wouldn't mind."

Picking up our things, Jimmy, Mitch, Melody, Paul, and I traipsed up the dirt path as we followed after the two star-crossed lovers and returned to Billy Bardem's house.

"Do I get to have a gun?" Melody asked.

"No!" we all shouted in chorus.

"Yeah, we're not insane," Mitch said, eyeing Melody suspiciously.

Mel casually shrugged and continued tagging along, perfectly content to be a part of the group. Getting her hands on some weapons was just a bonus.

Before continuing the rest of the way to Billy's house to resupply, I paused and turned to look back at Fort Liberty one last time. The powerful tree trunks of the mighty oak and dogwoods that had kept us safe from the blue menace from outer space had been mauled half to death. Its bark was shredded, claw marks carved into its meaty trunks, and blue, glowing slime beleaguered the ground like fluorescent silly string after a rave.

In twenty-four hours, we'd had a brush with death and came out the other side, not as imaginary Lords of Summer, but as real men. At least one of us had, that is. He'd beheld the glory and beauty of his first real woman, received his first real kiss, and given us all hope. Billy Bardem wasn't just my best friend; he was an outright legend.

I'm sure that wherever Billy's dad was now, he was looking down on his son with all the pride and joy in the world. Of that, I was certain.

On the distant horizon, more meteors streaked across the sky as they darted to every part of the world. Just like the one that crashed into the woods behind Billy Bardem's house, they all had purple glowing tails. This is how we knew it was a full-on invasion.

Together, we'd gotten into the biggest pickle of our lives, but together, we managed to survive to tell about it. And now we knew how to fight back. With the sky full of orange flaming rocks with purple dust trails, I knew this would be one of the weirdest summers of our lives.

1986
EPILOGUE

WE COULD HARDLY BELIEVE OUR EYES WHEN we emerged from the woods, returning home to find half the town gathered in Billy Bardem's backyard. The Kims, Mr. McIntyre, his wife Eve, and Paul's parents, Larry and Tanya Anders, were there. Even their cousin Drake and his two Rottweilers, Rocky and Bullwinkle, stood together by the back patio picnic table.

Anyone who knew anyone on our side of town had convened here—at ground zero—the first meteor strike and alien sighting. That's when I heard Mel's voice squeak, "Mom?"

Sure enough, our own mother was there, too, and she was sitting next to Billy's mom at the old green picnic table. Instead of a barbecue with food laid out, however, the table had an array of guns, ammunition, and extra cartridges splayed across it.

Our mom was loading bullets into cartridges as if she were one of the French Resistance soldiers of

World War II. Needless to say, I had a lot of questions.

Upon hearing Mel's voice, she stopped what she was doing and looked up—a wide smile forming on her lips. "Oh, thank God, you're both safe," she said, setting down what she was working on. She promptly raced over to us and drew us both into her arms, giving us the biggest hugs of our lives.

"Ah, Mom," I said in embarrassment. "The guys are all watching."

"You think I care?" she replied. And then, to add insult to the injury, along with the massive weight of crippling embarrassment, she repeatedly kissed both of our heads. Melody merely giggled, and I finally gave in to Mom's over-affectionate display of her love for us and let it happen.

Once she finally let go of us, she looked over at Sarah and said, "Thank you for keeping my babies safe."

"Actually, Mrs. Mahoney... it was the other way around. They saved me." Sarah turned and winked at us. I nodded, and Melody went over to take Sarah's hand.

"The whole neighborhood's gotta be here," Mitch said as we scanned all the faces. It seems Billy's mom had rallied the troops, and the base of operations was Billy "Backwoods" Bardem's house. And for perhaps the first time in twenty-four hours, none of us felt afraid.

"What's going on, Mom?" I asked.

The scratchy sound of a Zippo lighter flint spitting up sparks drew our attention to Billy's mom, Caroline, lighting a fresh cigarette.

"In case you kids haven't noticed," she said in her raspy manner, puffing the cigarette to life between her thin, chapped lips, "but there's an alien invasion underway."

"Oh, believe you me, Mrs. Bardem," Paul said, pushing his glasses up on his nose for the umpteenth time. "We know."

Caroline nodded and then turned back to her son. "Now, Billy, you get some of your brother's pistols and teach your lil' friends here how to shoot proper like. Looks like we'll be needing all hands on deck for this one."

"Yes, ma'am," Billy said with a smile that only grew bigger as he looked at me. My eyes widened as I shot him a perplexed look, but he merely walked over to the picnic table and picked up a nine-millimeter

Glock handgun. Then, he turned to us all, and pulling back on the slide, he cocked the gun. "So, who's first?"

We all exchanged glances, and it dawned on me what Billy had been getting at. I raised my hand and signaled to the others what would happen next, and like a sports team in perfect harmony, they all nodded in acknowledgement. At the same time, in one fluid motion, we deliberately withdrew from the line, taking one large step back. Everyone moved back as a group, leaving only my sister, Melody, standing out in front.

Billy looked down at her and smiled, her large green eyes looking back up at him, a smile on her face.

"I was only twelve when my dad taught me how to shoot. So, I'd be happy to teach you to shoot, if that's okay."

"Is it okay?" Melody asked, "Are you shitting me? Hell, yeah, it's okay!"

"Language!" my mom yelled.

"Sorry, Mom!" Melody answered.

Billy released the cartridge, pulled the slide all the way back until it jettisoned the bullet, which he expertly caught mid-air, and then, having safely disarmed the gun, he slapped the firearm into

Melody's outstretched hands.

We all cheered as Melody's wish had finally come true. She'd gotten her gun. And for everyone who knew her, that was as terrifying as it was exciting. Those aliens didn't even know what was coming, the poor unsuspecting saps. In that moment, I almost felt sorry for them. Almost.

"May God help us all," Mitch said, letting out a nervous chuckle.

"May God help those poor alien bastards is what I think you meant to say," Paul retorted.

"Yeah, what 'The Brain' said," Jimmy chimed in.

Everyone looked at my sister with trepidation and fear, everyone but me, Billy, and Sarah. We all knew the truth. If anyone was going to survive the end of the world, it was going to be my little sister. That was an undeniable, incontrovertible fact.

TO BE CONTINUED IN:

THE LORDS OF SUMMER INVASION

1986

BONUS CHAPTER: THE TERROR AT MAKE-OUT POINT

SARAH LEWIS AND THE WOODRIDGE HIGH Cougars had just won the National High School Cheerleading Competition. To celebrate, her boyfriend, Dean Westfall, took her out to Saddle Creek Steakhouse, a fancy restaurant at the Saddle Club near the Woodridge fairgrounds and racetrack.

Sarah ordered a steak, cooked medium-rare, with a fully loaded baked potato, while Dean had a burger with onions, fries, a pickle wedge, and a Dr. Pepper.

Naturally, after dinner, Dean came up with the bright idea that they needed fresh air and privacy to digest all that meat, and so he took her to Make-Out Point, which sat out of town. From the vantage point on the hill where the teenagers all liked to convene, you could see that Woodridge River sat on one side while the state forest sat on the other.

When they arrived at the spot, three other cars were already parked there. The car windows were all steamed up from whatever activities the young people were doing, but Sarah had a good idea of the sorts of things teens got up to at a place called Make-Out Point. It wasn't rocket science, after all.

Sarah blushed, secretly anticipating what Dean had brought her here for, and she rolled down the window to help cool herself down.

As they sat together in the car, not talking, she nervously brushed her skirt down as Dean put the car in park and turned the radio down just as the song 'Paradise by the Dashboard Light' by Meatloaf began to play. He looked over at her and nervously ran his fingers through his hair.

"I—"

"It—" they both began simultaneously.

They laughed nervously, and then Sarah replied, "You go."

"No, you," Dean replied with a chuckle. "I insist."

"Okay, then. I, was, um, just going to say that it

looks busy tonight."

Dean looked out at several other cars lining up along the edge of the riverbank. He nodded and said, "Yeah, I guess everyone is bringing their girl here tonight for some…"

Dean's voice trailed off as he shot Sarah an embarrassed look.

"Some… what?" she probed, smiling and biting her bottom lip in a flirtatious way that she knew would get his heart racing.

"You know what," he said.

She punched him lightly on the arm. "Tell me!"

"For some, *you know*," he repeated in a low whisper, still too nervous to actually come out and say it.

Sarah laughed and leaned back against the door armrest. Gently reaching down, she pinched the pleats of her skirt and, slowly yet deliberately, began to pull her hemline up until her entire leg was prominently on display.

Dean gulped nervously. "We can find another location if it's too crowded for you," he offered.

"Do I look bothered?" asked Sarah, still chewing seductively on her bottom lip. Her smooth leg basked in the light of the dashboard—an idea she'd gotten from listening to the song.

"I guess not," replied Dean. He was beginning to sweat profusely, which made Sarah laugh.

"Hey, it's all right," she said, leaning forward and placing her hand on his thigh. "I wouldn't have come out here with you if I didn't want to be here. Just take a deep breath and relax. It'll be okay. I promise." She then dug her nails into his leg and squeezed, getting him to sit upright with surprise. "I don't bite…much," she teased. She pawed at the air like a cat and then leaned back and laughed some more.

Dean nodded. Leaning forward, he reached across Sarah's chest, barely grazing her with his arm as he opened the glove box and drew out a pack of smokes.

"Since when did you start smoking?" asked Sarah.

Dean tapped the pack against his palm and watched as a single cigarette slid up out of the opening. Kissing it out with his lips, he patted himself down to try to find his lighter.

"Don't worry," Sarah said, holding up the lighter in her hands. "I've got it."

She flicked the flint wheel on the Zippo lighter,

and it sparked and kicked up a flame. She lit Dean's cigarette and then clapped the Zippo's lid shut, snuffing out the flame. Leaning back in the seat, she watched him roll down his window partway and blow a stream of smoke out the crack. "I don't know. About a year ago. I've been trying not to do it around you, because I know you've been training so hard for regionals."

"Well, that's why I love you," Sarah said. "You're considerate and you think of me even when I'm gone. That means a lot."

Dean tapped the cigarette on the edge of his window and watched the ash fall past his glass and flutter away on the breeze. "That's because I have the best girlfriend in the world," he replied. "Why wouldn't I think of you all the time?"

"What are you thinking right now?" Sarah drew her skirt up even more, to the point of it being impossible to pull it up any further. Dean looked down at her golden tan legs and gulped.

He took another long drag and then blew the smoke out of the car before replying. "You know you drive me wild, baby," he said, leaning forward. Dean placed a palm on the seat directly between her thighs, and Sarah scooted up against the car door as he leaned in to kiss her.

"Heh-hemmm..." she cleared her throat and eyed his cigarette, still smoldering between his fingers of his free hand.

"Oh... right," he said. Flicking the cigarette out her window, it whizzed by her head, but she kept her gaze locked on his beautiful brown eyes.

Reaching up, she grabbed the collar of his shirt and pulled him into her. Their lips touched, and they kissed. The evening's cool air washed over them, and Dean looked into Sarah's ocean blue eyes and smiled.

"What?" she laughed, timidly. Brushing a tuft of blonde hair out of her eyes, she waited for his reply.

"You're a good kisser," he said.

"I know," Sarah laughed. When he didn't move in to neck her like she'd expected, she touched his shoulder. "Is anything wrong?"

"It's just that... I mean, we've been seeing each other for roughly five months now, and kissing is all we ever do."

"And you're wondering if we could..."

"Do something a little more."

Sarah sat up and sighed. "You know my parents

are strict about this kind of stuff. They're super religious. It can be a bit much. But if I go all the way, I want it to be..." She paused, realizing that what she was about to say would start a fight. She liked Dean. She liked him a lot. But she wasn't sure she was "in love" with him.

"You want it to be special," he said, answering for her.

She nodded. It wasn't exactly what she intended to say but, at least this way, they wouldn't need to have a fight or break up over her considering the possibility that *Mr. Right* was still out there somewhere and inadvertently breaking Dean's heart by implying that he wasn't the one she was destined to be with.

"Maybe we'll get there when we get there," Sarah answered, smiling coquettishly. "Just don't expect it to be tonight."

Dean let out a disgruntled sigh and then said, "Okay." Looking into her blue eyes, he asked, "Can we at least keep kissing?"

She laughed as she grabbed Dean by the scruff of his neck and drew him in for a long, sultry kiss. Coming up for air, she replied, "You bet. After all, I have it on good authority that I'm a great kisser."

Dean laughed. "You don't say?"

They hadn't even gotten another minute into necking when they were suddenly interrupted by a thunderous boom that shook their car.

"What in blazes was that?" Dean asked, sitting up.

All the other high schoolers got out of their cars and looked up at the sky. Streaks of fire rained down all around them. Ash and smoldering fragments of what they could only assume were meteorites landed in the forest behind them, kicking up dirt and debris and scorching the tree tops, which glowed bright orange as they smoldered like the glowing embers of a campfire.

"That must have hit a quarter mile from here," Dean said excitedly, opening his door and stepping out of his 1979 Pontiac Firebird Trans Am with the iconic "Screaming Chicken" painted in gold on its hood.

"Are you sure it's safe to get out of the car?" Sarah asked, peering up at the sky. "There might be more meteors."

Dean glanced up only briefly and then said, "I don't see anything." Then, turning toward Sarah, he reached out his hand. "You coming or what?"

Sarah laughed. "You're tripping if you think I'm going out there to find some toxic nuclear space rock with you."

"Come on," Dean pleaded. "It'll be fun."

Sarah sighed and, reluctantly, got out of the car and followed him to the edge of the parking lot. There was already a gathering of onlookers peering out at the crash site. Dean and Sarah came up alongside everyone and stood beneath a sky full of falling stars. Luckily, the rest of the meteor shower was too far away to be of any danger to any of them.

Sarah couldn't help but feel this would almost be romantic if it weren't for all the others crowding around to get a look at the impact crater left by the nearby meteor strike.

"Hey, it might be cool to head down there and check it out," Dean insisted. Looking around, he saw Michael Whitmore and Timothy Urkoski already leaving their girlfriends behind to go investigate the crash site.

Dean looked back at Sarah, as if to ask permission to join the guys in a bit of adventure and exploration.

"Don't you dare think of leaving me for some extraterrestrial space debris, Dean Westfall. You hear me?"

Sarah stamped her foot and crossed her arms, shooting Dean a disapproving gaze.

"Pretty please?" he begged. "I'll make it up to you when I get back."

"Oh, really?" Sarah asked skeptically. "How?"

"How?" he repeated, scratching his head in contemplation. It was clear he hadn't actually thought it through.

"I don't know. All I know is that Mike and Tim have already entered the forest, and I'm still stuck here arguing with you."

"This isn't an argument," Sarah said, quickly losing her patience. "This is a conversation. But if I'm not more interesting to you than some dumb space rock, maybe you should go out there. I'll just walk home." Sarah turned and began to storm off, heading to the entrance of the parking area.

"Wait!" Dean said, jogging up to her and grabbing her arm. "Just take a moment."

Sarah stopped and, folding her arms across her chest again, looked at him. "I'm listening."

"I'm sorry," Dean said. "You're right. You are more important to me than some stupid space rock."

"And?" Sarah probed, fishing for more than a barely thought-out apology.

"And… uh… I want to go back to the car and make out some more?" Dean's voice quivered as though he was unsure of his own answer.

"Good answer," Sarah said, smiling cheerfully. Taking Dean's hand in hers, she turned around and skipped back toward the car, towing him behind her.

Just then, screams echoed from the tree line where Mike and Tim had just entered moments earlier. Sarah and Dean stopped in their tracks and turned to face the forest. Before anyone could react, Tim came running out of the trees, screaming something.

"Start the car! Start the car!" he shouted.

Tina, his girlfriend, nodded and ran to the car, hopped into the driver's seat, and searched for the keys. Unable to find them, she got back out and shouted, "Where are the keys?"

"Oh, crap," Tim said, patting down his pockets as he ran. Fishing out the keys, he paused long enough to throw them. Everyone watched the keys sail through the air—as if in slow motion—and land at Tina's feet. She bent down to pick them up and was about to run back to the car when Mike, the other guy who'd gone into the woods, stumbled out of the forest.

Something wasn't right, though. Mike staggered forward, then stopped, then staggered forward again. He seemed off-balance—discombobulated somehow.

Everything grew silent as Mike had come to a complete standstill and stood frozen approximately twenty feet from the forest's edge.

"What's he doing?" asked Jennifer Nakamura, Ryan Coolidge's girlfriend, as she climbed down from Ryan's red Jeep Wrangler with thirty-five-inch wheels and a five-inch lift kit. Ryan, who stood beside her, shook his head.

"I have no idea, babe."

"Hey, man," Dean called out. "You all right?"

But there was no answer. Mike just stood there, as though he were in shock and couldn't move.

"Wait, I have an idea," said Ryan. He turned and jumped back into his Jeep, flipped on the auxiliary switches, and lit up the spotlight attachments mounted to the rollbar.

Meanwhile, Jennifer Nakamura, the only Asian in our senior class, stood in front of the beams of light and pointed at something further out. "Over there!"

Everyone turned to see Mike standing in a pool of blood. His own blood. It dripped down his chin and throat, and that was when Sarah and the others noticed it. Mike's right arm was torn clean off.

Abby Sayers, Mike's girlfriend, let out a horrendous scream at the terrible sight of him. This caught Mike's ear, and he looked up. Upon seeing Abby's face, something clicked. Blood and gore saturating his shirt, he mumbled, "Run." When it became apparent that nobody had heard his words, he shouted, "Run, goddammit! Run!!!"

Tim dashed over to his 1969 fastback Mustang just as Tina had started the engine. He dove in through the passenger window and slid into the seat, yelling, "Go, go, go!"

The Mustang's tires kicked up dirt and sand as it shot backward in reverse, but before Tina could shift it into drive, something flew out of the trees and landed on the hood of the car.

Tina looked up and screamed. A creature, unlike anything any of them had ever seen before, stood staring at them through the cracked windshield, its massive jowls dripping with blue slime.

It looked like a giant panther, but with six green

eyes and an elongated, alligator-like snout with lacerating teeth. Whatever it was, Sarah thought, it was hideous looking. In addition to having the face of a Velociraptor, it also had a leathery hide, comparable to a rhinoceros, but it was as black as a panther at the stroke of midnight. If its ability to blend into the night wasn't terrifying enough, its nine long tails stretched long and thin like bullwhips, the ends of which had large purplish feathers, and each feather, as sharp as an arrowhead carved from obsidian, was dabbed with a blue tip that glowed like fireflies in the night.

Sarah recoiled in fright, and Dean, wasting no time, sprang into action, grabbed her arm, and pulled her back toward the car. "We've gotta get out of here," he said.

Sarah looked back over her shoulder as Dean dragged her along behind him. "What in God's name is it?"

"I don't know," Dean answered. "All I know is I'm not going to wait around to find out."

Sarah covered her mouth as the creature's tails whipped spastically about as if they were searching for something—or someone—to latch on to. She watched in horror as six of the tails wrapped around the

Mustang and pierced the open windows. As the myriad of tails' arrowhead-like tips penetrated the vehicle, they sliced both Tim and Tina's necks. Blood gurgled out of their gaping wounds as they gasped their last breath. Once the life had drained out of them, their bodies slumped back onto the car seat. Strangely, they sat in the car normally, their open eyes staring vacantly out at the creature as blood continued to gush from the slits on their necks.

Sarah covered her mouth and stifled a scream. She'd never seen anybody die in front of her own eyes before. And now three people were dead.

The beast turned, metal crunching beneath its dense weight, the roof of the Mustang crumpling in as it entombed the two corpses stuck inside. As it looked around at the remaining kids, it growled a low, menacing growl, challenging the human creatures for dominance.

Ryan Coolidge sprang up and threw a rock at it. The rock hit it in the side of the neck, and the creature spun to face Ryan just as he swas picking up another rock. "You killed Tim, you ugly mother-fu—"

Ryan's admonitions were cut off mid-sentence when the beast leaped off the car and onto the ground five feet in front of him. "Whoa, there… big guy," Ryan said, dropping his rock and raising both hands as he slowly backed up. "I didn't mean anything by it."

"I don't think he understands you," whispered Abby.

"I know that," Ryan whispered back. "But if I stay calm, he'll stay calm."

"I don't think that's how it works," she replied.

He waved at her to stay back when the alien shifted a couple of steps to the side and growled as it circled them. Ryan, standing in front of Abby, placed himself between her and the beast. The moment she saw an opportunity, however, she turned and ran toward the dirt road, screaming for her life.

"What are you doing?!" Jennifer called out from the Jeep as she watched Abby run away as fast as she could.

If only she had been quieter, Sarah thought, then the beast would have focused on Ryan instead of her. But her hysterical wailing caused the beast to snap its head in her direction.

Like a cat chasing a mouse, it couldn't resist, and the monster sprang from vehicle to vehicle, bounding away as it chased her. Abby's screams were abruptly stifled when the creature pounced on her, slamming her into the ground and crushing her. Sarah shuddered when she heard the snap, crackle, and pop of Abby's ribcage giving way.

The creature sniffed Abby's neck and head, its slimy jowls pressing blue glowing goop into her hair. Abby coughed up dirt and turned her head, desperately gasping for breath. Her eyes watered from the pain as she craned her neck to the side to get a better look at the thing standing over her. But it was too late; by the time her eyes met its black, obsidian gaze, its fangs were already bearing down on her.

There was a loud crunch as the creature chomped down on Abby's head, her skull getting crushed between its razor-sharp teeth. At the same time, her right eyeball bulged from the pressure and then popped like a grape. Sarah watched in abject terror as blood oozed out of Abby's eye socket, nostrils, and ears. Abby mumbled some random words, but her brain was already so badly damaged that only a confused jumble of nonsense escaped her lips.

The monster shook Abby's limp body about like a coyote shaking a rabbit ensnared in its jaws, and her limp body flopped around like a lifeless rag doll. As this was happening, Ryan Coogler grabbed the telescoping radio antenna on his jeep, snapped it off, and proceeded to run up to the alien and whip its face while shouting, "You killed her, you stinking piece of..."

"Ryan!" Jennifer shouted. "Get away from it. She's already dead!"

Sarah agreed with Jen. There was no reason to try to save Abby because she was already a goner.

An unnatural sound, wet and thick, emanated from Ryan's gut—a kind of *shuh—hurk*. Sarah and Jen watched in dismay as Ryan looked down to find that three of the creature's razor-tipped tails had penetrated his torso.

"No!" Jen screamed as she watched Ryan stagger back and drop the car antenna. "Not today," she said as she slid out of the side of the Jeep, grabbing the baseball bat from behind the passenger seat.

Jen gripped the bat tightly in her hands and marched toward the beast. She cracked her neck side to side like boxers do before a fight and screamed, "Let my boyfriend go, you piece of crap alien!"

Her long black hair swayed behind her as she charged forward. She had on tattered jean shorts and a white ACDC t-shirt tied in a knot at the waist, which gave her a hardcore girl rock vibe. The fact that she had tattoos on both arms, one of an oriental dragon and the other a heart with a banderole featuring Ryan's name, gave Sarah all the confidence in the world that, out of anybody here tonight, Jen was the only one who might stand a fighting chance of getting out of this alive.

Winding up, Jen took wide, powerful swings and managed to get a couple of solid hits in before the creature grew annoyed and, like a bucking bronco, kicked her in the chest and sent her flying backward.

Jen crashed into Sarah, her head knocking against Sarah's as they both smashed into Dean's car. Sarah's back slammed into the passenger side mirror, eliciting a scream, and the rearview mirror snapped off from the force of the hit.

At the same time, Jen's head collided with the top edge of the car door with a resounding crack, and she was instantly knocked unconscious. Both girls collapsed to the ground, winded, fighting to regain consciousness.

Vision blurred, Sarah managed to stay conscious and looked over to find Dean dragging Jen by her ankles to get her away from the creature. Realizing she hadn't breathed in half a minute, Sarah gulped and sucked in a giant breath of air, her lungs wheezing as she leaned to the side. The hit had knocked the wind clean out of her.

Smashing into cars with its body, the alien barked and honked as it grew agitated by the bright lights of the vehicles. It whipped its myriad of tails all about in a flurried dance—their barbed ends shattering the remaining headlights. Glass shot everywhere, and Dean rolled Jen's unconscious body under the Jeep as the Jeep spotlights exploded overhead.

Having stashed Jennifer safely under the Jeep, Dean turned around only to find himself standing face-to-face with the beast. He froze in his tracks and gulped. With his back pinned against the Jeep, there was nowhere to run.

Sarah wanted to shout out at the top of her lungs and warn him not to try anything stupid. The monster was too strong, and it had already decimated everything that had come for it. Running away would be the better option. She had confidence that he was faster than Abby and stood a better chance of keeping ahead of the creature.

She flopped onto her back and rolled under the Trans Am. Turning her head, she made eye contact with Jen, who was waking up only to find herself lying beneath the Jeep's axle, but protected by its massive off-road tires. She couldn't see Dean, but she didn't need to. Because, at that moment, he screamed out a fierce battle cry and then was immediately silenced as the creature disemboweled him.

Blood rained down onto Jen, who flinched as Dean's body fell to the ground in two separate pieces next to her. Sarah watched from beneath the car, eyes flooding with tears, as the creature bent down and sniffed Dean's lifeless body. She clasped her hands over her mouth to stifle her sobs and thought to herself, *Don't move. Don't move.*

Meanwhile, Jen had no such luck. The alien heard Jen's whimpering and began to sniff around the Jeep, looking for where the sound was coming from. Jen and Sarah's eyes met again, both red from tears, and Sarah put her finger to her lips and gestured for Jen to stay quiet.

Jen nodded in silence as the alien pawed at a patch of dirt and stuck its head down between the tires to try to see who was under there. It snorted and puffed air through its nostrils, jostling Jen's hair. Instead of waiting for it to find her, she managed to roll away and pop out the other side of the Jeep. Somehow, she forced herself up to her feet and didn't waste any time standing around. She immediately darted toward the nearby trees.

The creature bit into the large Jeep tire, deflating it. It pulled and stretched the rubber, shaking it slightly, but realizing it wasn't what it wanted. As it heard the crunch of footsteps on dry twigs and grass, it looked up only to catch a glimpse of Jen's back before she disappeared into a grove of trees.

Howling, it grew restless and kicked the Jeep to the side, causing it to skid into the Trans Am. The two vehicles slammed together, and Sarah covered her head, rolled to the side, and curled into a ball to avoid getting squashed by the wheels. Once she realized she was safe, she crawled out from underneath the car and cautiously got up. Through the windows opposite her, she watched the creature bound after Jen, almost playful in its pursuit, like a cat toying with a mouse before pouncing.

Sarah felt a sense of relief seeing that Jen had made it to the woods and disappeared into a grove of trees. It was dark, so maybe she'd have a fighting chance by ditching the beast in the cover of the dense forest.

As the creature loped off, Sarah let out a sigh of relief and immediately felt a sharp sting running across the whole of her abdomen. It was more than just a stitch in her side; it was a sharp, lacerating pain, and she looked down to find a large, gushing wound on her stomach, her cheerleader uniform shredded and bloody.

During all the commotion, one of the creature's tails had lacerated her lower abdomen. The edges of the cut glowed purple, like the beast's luminescent hide, and the strange glow seemed to seep into her skin. The cut wasn't lethal, but it stung like a son of a gun.

Reaching down, Sarah touched her wound and winced. The pain was unbelievably sharp. She'd cut her finger on a cutting knife before, so she knew that it wasn't like that. It wasn't metal or shrapnel from the damaged cars. But a couple of summers back, she'd gone to Florida with her family, and she'd been stung by jellyfish. This sting felt more severe than that, so she could only surmise that she must have been sliced open by one of that thing's razor-blade tails.

She groaned, and slowly, everything blurred out of focus. Growing dizzy, she prayed for Jen to make a clean getaway. She couldn't bear the thought of being the only survivor of the Make-Out Point Massacre.

Sarah stepped over dead bodies and severed limbs as she navigated the carnage lying all around her. She thought about how much she loved Dean, and a single tear trickled out of the corner of her eye as she realized perhaps she'd been too hasty to judge how she'd felt. Maybe he had been the one all along, and it had taken the act of losing him for her to realize it.

She wiped the tears from her cheeks with her thumb and then, clutching her stomach, made her way to the forest's edge. She paused to listen, and the creature's ferocious noises grew fainter and fainter. All she had to do was go in the opposite direction as it was, and she'd have a surviving chance of making it out of this ordeal alive.

Sarah stepped into the thick of the trees and walked for what seemed like hours. It probably had been. That's when she heard something peculiar. She came to a standstill to listen and, sure enough, she heard the sound of children talking. Not only that, but she could make out a flashlight in the middle of the woods going on and off, lighting up the green pines, then going dark, only to light everything up again.

What are you idiots doing? she wondered. But, if they didn't know about the monster in the woods, if they weren't aware of what kind of danger they were in... *oh, crap.* This was going to be bad. Maybe even worse than what happened to her friends.

She had to warn them. She had to reach them before the creature did and get them to safety. If she could prevent another massacre, then maybe Dean's sacrifice wouldn't have been for nothing. If she could save them, then it would mean that he gave his life so that she'd escape with hers—and in so doing—give her a chance to rescue these kids.

Groaning in pain, Sarah grabbed her abdomen and turned toward the flashing lights, and began limping through the woods. Even though she felt like she'd been run through a meat grinder, she knew she was the only one who could warn the kids of the danger they were in.

Editor's Note:

*This story picks up in *The Lords of Summer* novella*

Published by Regolith Publications © 2025

ABOUT THE AUTHOR

Tristan Vick is a multi-genre author specializing in science fiction, fantasy, and horror, and has also dabbled in mystery and suspense. He graduated from Montana State University with degrees in English Literature and Asian Cultural Studies and speaks fluent Japanese. He lives with his wife and three children in Japan. When he's not commuting on the train or teaching English, he spends his time reading, writing, binge-watching his favorite television shows, and eating sara-udon. In addition to being traditionally published, Tristan Vick continues to self-publish under his imprint, Regolith Publications, LLC, and Regolith Comics. His comic book series, The Astonishing Adventures of Alicia Carter & Robot, has sold over 10,000 copies in its first year of release. His other comic book works include Daughter of Wolves, The Profane, Blood & Chrome, The Viking Berserker Zarna, and Animal Woman.